Mr. Pipes

Comes to America

Douglas Bond

Christian Liberty Press
Arlington Heights, Illinois

Published by
Christian Liberty Press
502 West Euclid Avenue
Arlington Heights, Illinois 60004
www.christianlibertypress.com

General editorship by Michael J. McHugh
Layout and editing by Edward J. Shewan
Copyediting by Carol H. Blair and Belit Shewan
Cover design by Bob Fine and graphics by Christopher D. Kou
Cover image by Dawn Doughty
Story images by Ron Ferris

Hymns are reprinted from the *Trinity Hymnal* (Copyright © 1961, 1990, Great Commission Publications). Used by permission.

ISBN 978-1-930367-53-1
        1-930367-53-8

Printed in the United States of America

Table of Contents

Mr. Pipes Comes to America

by Douglas Bond

Author of
Mr. Pipes and the British Hymn Makers
and
Mr. Pipes and Psalms and Hymns of the Reformation

Preface

Mr. Pipes Comes to America continues the story about two young Americans and their friend Mr. Pipes. It is a story about the most important subject in the world—the worship of Almighty God.

The worship of God in modern times has too often become shallow and man-centered. Many Christians at the opening of the Twenty-first Century, including young believers, have never understood the importance of approaching God with awesome reverence and majestic praise. As readers move through *Mr. Pipes Comes to America*, however, they will not only learn about the fascinating lives of famous hymn writers, but will also be encouraged to cultivate an attitude of humble adoration as they approach their Maker.

Young Christians who grasp the significance of what they read will come to the wonderful realization that their worship is connected with the Church universal—the followers of Christ throughout the world, both past and present. In other words, young readers will understand that true worship is not isolated from believers of the past but is, rather, built upon their godly traditions.

Perhaps the greatest tradition of true biblical worship, aside from scriptural exposition and prayer, is the holy exercise of hymn singing. It is, therefore, the express purpose of this book to rekindle a genuine interest within the lives of young believers in the traditional hymns of the faith once delivered unto the saints. May God be pleased to use this little volume to revive an interest in and appreciation for that which is true and praiseworthy in the realm of Christian worship.

Michael J. McHugh

For Brittany, Rhodri, Cedric, and Desmond

"A good hymn is the best use
to which poetry can be devoted."

John Greenleaf Whittier

"Good music for worship is a moral issue…. The eternal
gospel cannot be commended with disposable, fashionable
music styles, otherwise there is the implication that the
gospel itself is somehow disposable and temporary."

Ralph Vaughan Williams
Preface to The English Hymnal, *1906*

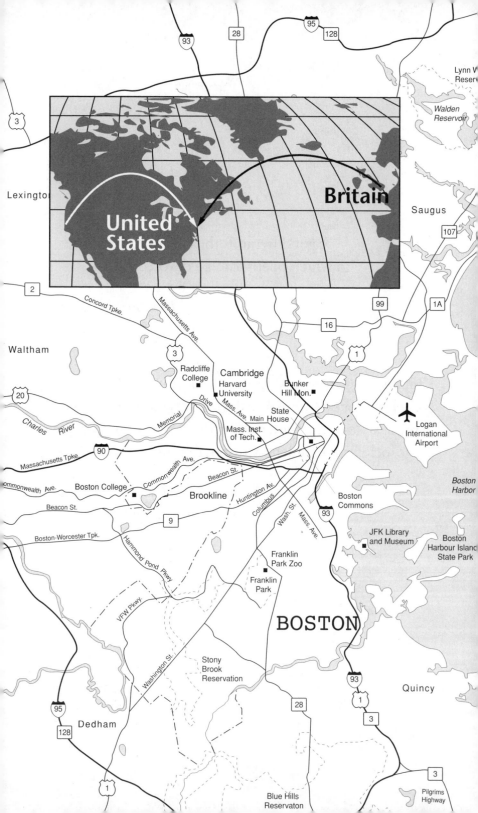

Chapter One

Simply Out of the Question!

First, Pilgrims Psalms in praise of God did raise,
And some high hymns did write in human phrase.
Then, worship's consumed in "revival" fire;
Now with a bee and a bop we raise God's ire.

"I say, old chap," said the white-haired man resting his arm comfortably on the tiller of his little black sailboat. "I say, what loveliness surrounds us on the Great Ouse today." The sunlight shone on his sprawling eyebrows as he turned his face upward and breathed deeply of the late November air. "Unseasonable loveliness, that is what I call it."

His companion made no reply but, twitching his whiskers, he turned toward the old man and blinked his staring green eyes several times.

"Yes, yes, m'Lord, though a bit cool," continued the man, his breath coming in wisps and puffs as he spoke, "'tis a lovely day— and a most successful one. The catch basket overflows with barbel, gentle breezes fill *Toplady's* sail, and the cottage lies around the bend—ah, yes, and a steaming cup of tea awaits." He steadied the tiller with his elbow and blew on his hands, rubbing them briskly together.

His companion only licked his lips and blinked as the old man nudged the tiller to starboard and eased off the mainsheet, adjusting the trim of the brick-colored sail.

"There, now," he said, resuming his reclining position at the stern. The mast and sail brushed lightly against the leafless branches of a willow tree drooping over the river. Empty rook nests cluttered the higher branches, and a tardy coot—disturbed by the boat—rose with a squeak and a flutter from the meadow

1

grass along the banks. The man sighed a contented and apprecia-tive sigh and began humming. After several moments, his hum-ming grew words: "All praise to God, who reigns above, the God of all creation...." His clear voice rose above the rustling and pat-tering of the river.

The twin arches of the Olney Bridge came slowly into view; and, through the willows, the ancient spire of the parish church pointed heavenward. The bells of the steeple slowly chimed the hour, echoing along the little valley.

Through all of this, his companion said not a word.

Now, if you were a water rat or a hedgehog sniffing and wad-dling near your hole along the riverbank, you might have cocked your fuzzy head to one side at the congenial scene and at the voice of the old man humming and occasionally speaking to— well, to no one. Then, if you sniffed the air more carefully you might just have caught the scent of another furry creature—

—But, wait, the old man speaks again.

"There, now, m'Lord, the staithe comes into view. And, fancy that, Dr. Dudley waits to receive us—a pleasant and welcome surprise." Turning toward shore he called, "Hello, Martin. De-lighted to see you."

Throwing the tiller to starboard, the old man steered in a tight circle. The sail luffed as he headed into the wind; moments later he nudged the boat against the stone pier.

A tall, dark-haired man wearing a well-tailored herringbone suit, stood with arms crossed and chin jutted, looking down at the mariners. The old man shipped the unused oars, released the halyard, and neatly folded the sail along the boom.

"Dr. Dudley, my dear fellow—you simply must stay for sup-per." He held open the catch basket as if to tempt his friend.

"Humph!" replied Dr. Dudley with a sniff. "I'm not one to interfere, as you well know." He cleared his throat. "However, I would be remiss in not observing the inherent dangers connected with maritime exploits—especially, my dear man, at your age and station in life." Here the man paused, took two wraps of his moustache around his index finger, and pulled viciously. "Mr.

Pipes, dear fellow, as your physician I simply must recommend engagements more suited to your—well, to your frailties."

"Frailties, indeed, dear fellow," replied Mr. Pipes with a good-natured chuckle as he made fast the mooring lines. "Weaknesses I have aplenty, but surely you, good doctor, must commend the virtue of outdoor exercise, judiciously engaged—surely you must."

"Of course, my dear man," replied the doctor. He grabbed his lapels and looked at the quiet waters of the river as if they were the final passage to the underworld. "But people *drown* in rivers, don't they. Besides, it's nearly December, and bitter cold! What's more, you've subjected Lord Underfoot—poor chap—to the dis-quieting deprivations of boating. You simply must have some consideration of others."

At this, Dr. Dudley bent over and patted the large head of Mr. Pipes' companion—an enormous gray cat showing considerable interest in the catch basket.

Mr. Pipes smiled mildly and said, "Yes, well, how about tea?"

◈ ◈ ◈

Once inside the cozy stone cottage, Lord Underfoot curled up on the hearth in front of the glowing coals, which Mr. Pipes soon coaxed into a snapping and spitting fire.

The companions dined at an oval table before the fire with both men offering choice pieces of fish to the eager Lord Under-foot, carefully stationed within reach. When only fish bones and crumbs of bread remained, and while the two sat sipping yet an-other cup of tea, Mr. Pipes cleared his throat and said:

"Well, now, I must tell you the latest news from America."

"America?"

"Yes."

"Must you?" groaned his companion.

"Indeed, I must," said Mr. Pipes with a good-natured laugh. "I've just received a most interesting letter from Annie and Drew—you do remember Annie and Drew, do you not?"

"Rather!" retorted Dr. Dudley, his chin poking upward. "Dashed impossible not to remember them, contributing as they have to your gallivanting adventures all of kingdom come."

As Mr. Pipes unfolded the letter, the fire crackled at their feet. He gazed at the letter for a moment, then setting it aside, he stood and warmed his hands before the fire as he continued.

"Delightful children, Martin, and you must know how very attached I have become to them." He paused, fingering the gilded frame holding a photograph of his late wife.

Dr. Dudley studied his elderly friend, an uncomprehending tilt to his head, but said nothing.

"I almost feel," continued Mr. Pipes, "as if God has given them to me to care for as my very own—in a manner of speaking, of course."

His head tilted still further, Dr. Dudley fidgeted with his moustache before replying.

"Charming, I am sure. But, if I may make so bold," he gestured toward the letter, "what is the substance of this communiqué from America?"

"Yes, yes, the letter," he picked up the letter; and, tapping it with the back of his hand, he went on. "Its essential message is quite direct—Americans can be that way, you understand."

"Indeed!" said Dr. Dudley, stomping his heel impatiently. "What is its essential message? Out with it, dear man."

"In the interest of directness, then—the children, and their parents, have invited me to visit for the Christmas holidays—though they call it 'vacation.'"

Dr. Dudley's teacup clattered onto its saucer, and his mouth gaped like an empty mailbox.

"In A-A-America?" he spluttered at last. "Utterly ridiculous—quite utterly ridiculous, of course, and naturally you've told them it's simply out of the question. Ha ha, your little joke, no doubt, now there's a good fellow."

"On the contrary, Martin," said Mr. Pipes. "In fact, I very much would like to see America."

"What? What?" Dr. Dudley's eyes grew round with astonishment. "I say, dear man, your family chose not to go to the beastly place in 16-whenever-it-was—I don't see how anything has materially changed since then. No, you simply must listen to reason and tell them the decision was made long ago and it is not your place to question your forefathers. It's out of your hands. That should settle it. Oh, Mr. Pipes, do be ruled by me in this matter, I beg you. What of the wild Indians—the buffalo stampedes—the hot dogs? A-and, Americans hate tea, you know."

Mr. Pipes smiled reassuringly. "I have reasoned it all out, my friend, and I simply must go—I *want* to go."

"Humph!" grunted Dr. Dudley, throwing his hands in the air and settling back into his chair. "You have taken leave of what I formerly considered to be the possession of a singular good sense. Gone now, forever, I fear." He leaned forward, clutching his hands together, and with concern on his face, continued, "You must think of your frailties—your health. You are not a young man anymore, my friend. Why, man, I am your physician and I must urge you—no, that's not strong enough—I *demand* that you give up this absurd, this infernal, this dashed insane notion!"

"I am to take that to mean you don't approve?" replied Mr. Pipes, the twitchings of a smile playing at the corners of his mouth.

"An old man, in your condition, *alone* in America? Of course I don't approve. No sane man would."

"Ah, Martin, I know it is your care for me that makes you reluctant—"

"I am not *reluctant*!" Dr. Dudley broke in.

"—That makes you ... cautious about my going."

"Nor am I *cautious*! I positively forbid it! One need not be cautious if one is not doing the thing."

"Ahem, yes," Mr. Pipes smiled at his friend. Lord Underfoot hopped onto the old man's lap and rumbled contentedly as Mr. Pipes stroked his charcoal fur. "How blessed am I to enjoy the ministrations of such a fine physician—and friend. Such considerations of my well-being invoke the deepest gratitude in my heart."

"There, now," said Dr. Dudley, a triumphant grin on his face. "I knew you would come round to my opinion at last."

"Well, yes. In a manner of speaking, I do see it your way," replied Mr. Pipes, taking another sip of tea. "I think yours is a simply marvelous idea—marvelous indeed."

"Idea?" Dr. Dudley looked confused. "To what idea, pray tell, are you referring?"

"Don't you remember? Oh, I remember your words most distinctly. It was in Geneva last summer, you insisted on accompanying me on my next adventure—those were your very words. And I am most grateful to you; I won't need to go *alone* to America. One of your finest ideas to date, indeed it is!"

"W-what!—did-did I—?" spluttered Dr. Dudley. "It is simply out of the question—out of the question!"

"Moreover, I accept," said Mr. Pipes with a decisive nod of his balding white head.

"Accept what?" groaned Dr. Dudley, holding his face in his hands.

"Your willingness to accompany me to America, of course. Annie and Drew wrote so very enthusiastically about our both coming—did I not mention it? And I've taken the liberty of purchasing two tickets from London to Boston—we leave in two weeks' time." Here the old man threw back his head and sang, "America, America, God shed his grace on thee!"

When Dr. Dudley found his voice, he slammed his palm on his knee and said, "Those little blighters!"

All Praise to God, Who Reigns Above

Let them give thanks to the LORD for his unfailing love and his wonderful deeds for men. Ps. 107:15

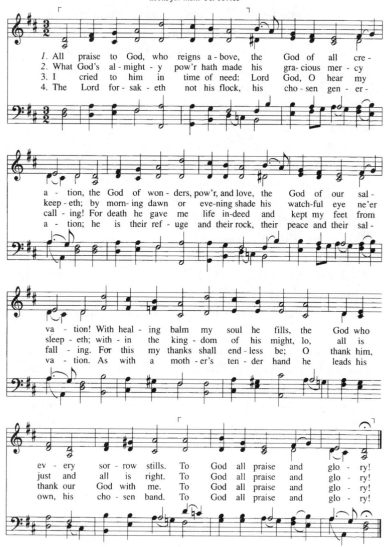

1. All praise to God, who reigns above, the God of all cre-
2. What God's al-might-y pow'r hath made his gra-cious mer-cy
3. I cried to him in time of need: Lord God, O hear my
4. The Lord for-sak-eth not his flock, his cho-sen gen-er-

a-tion, the God of won-ders, pow'r, and love, the God of our sal-
keep-eth; by morn-ing dawn or eve-ning shade his watch-ful eye ne'er
call-ing! For death he gave me life in-deed and kept my feet from
a-tion; he is their ref-uge and their rock, their peace and their sal-

va-tion! With heal-ing balm my soul he fills, the God who
sleep-eth; with-in the king-dom of his might, lo, all is
fall-ing. For this my thanks shall end-less be; O thank him,
va-tion. As with a moth-er's ten-der hand he leads his

ev-ery sor-row stills. To God all praise and glo-ry!
just and all is right. To God all praise and glo-ry!
thank our God with me. To God all praise and glo-ry!
own, his cho-sen band. To God all praise and glo-ry!

5. Ye who confess Christ's holy name, to God give praise and glory!
Ye who the Father's pow'r proclaim, to God give praise and glory!
All idols underfoot be trod, the Lord is God! The Lord is God!
To God all praise and glory!

6. Then come before his presence now and banish fear and sadness;
to your Redeemer pay your vow and sing with joy and gladness:
Though great distress my soul befell, the Lord, my God, did all things well.
To God all praise and glory!

Johann J. Schütz, 1675
Tr. by Frances E. Cox, 1864

MIT FREUDEN ZART 8.7.8.7.8.8.7.
Bohemian Brethren's *Gesangbuch*, 1566

Chapter Two

John Eliot and the Bay Psalm Book
1604–1690

The Lord to me a Shepherd is,
    Want therefore shall not I.
He in the folds of tender grass
    Doth cause me down to lie....

Meanwhile, the aforementioned Annie and Drew, with their mother and stepfather, made plans for what Drew described would be, "The best Christmas on the planet!"

When asked in a letter what he wanted to see in America, Mr. Pipes showed particular interest in the East: "... where your Pilgrims first landed and the surrounding colonial sites—I simply must see Plymouth—Plymouth, America, that is."

It was finally settled that Annie and Drew would fly to Boston and meet Mr. Pipes and Dr. Dudley the day school ended for Christmas vacation. After four days of sightseeing in the East, they would all fly to California to celebrate Christmas with Annie and Drew's parents. Not much time to see the colonial sites, but it couldn't be helped. "Your father," reasoned their mother, "will be busy finishing the Hutchinson deal right up till Christmas anyway, and I've got things I'm doing, of course. But, it can't be helped, you'll all come back here for Christmas."

"But ... only four days?" said Annie, desperate for more time.

"Hey," said Drew, "maybe this year we could just move Christmas to the thirtieth, instead of the twenty-fifth. *Say*, while we're at it, let's just move it to January thirtieth! That'd fix everything."

"*Drew*," said Annie. No, there was no way around it. A very short adventure lay ahead, and they'd just have to make the most of it.

❖ ❖ ❖

"*Colonials!*" screamed Dr. Dudley, as another horn blared and yet another driver raised a menacing fist while swerving to miss them.

Mr. Pipes gripped the dashboard and looked slightly pale while Annie and Drew scrunched low in the backseat, bracing for the worst.

"My dear fellow," remarked Mr. Pipes, a studied calmness in his voice, "I say, I do believe you might be attempting to drive on the wrong side of the general flow of traffic."

"Yes, yes," said Dr. Dudley, wiping his brow, his moustache twitching from side to side as he swerved across the lane. "Just because they're all doing it incorrectly [horns blaring] does not mean I must descend to their level—not I [screeching tires]. What's more, they've gone and plopped the steering wheel on the wrong side—those blundering *Colonials*! Can't they get anything right? Steering wheels belong on the right, traffic on the left [more horns]. Everyone knows that!"

"Your care of me o'er leaps itself," stammered Mr. Pipes, still gripping the dashboard.

"I-I've heard busses are really good in Boston," came Annie's muffled voice from under her winter coat, where she buried her face in case they crashed—which seemed likely.

Once on Route 3, with a solid wall of concrete keeping him on the right side of things, Dr. Dudley's driving grew more tolerable. After one more near-hit—almost running the car off the road—while scouring the road map, Mr. Pipes took the map and directed him through the streets of Plymouth, Massachusetts, to Water Street. The car screeched to a halt in a near-empty parking lot overlooking a broad bay.

"There, now," said Dr. Dudley, rapping the steering wheel. "I think I handled that rather nicely, if I do say so myself."

Mr. Pipes didn't reply, but
eagerly lifted the door
handle and stepped
into the cold air.
   "Get a load of
that!" said Drew, bolt-
ing from the car and
running to the edge
of the parking lot.
"It's a real ship—the
kind with sails!"
   "It's beauti-
ful," said Annie,
breathing in the cold
salt air as she joined her brother.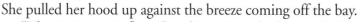
She pulled her hood up against the breeze coming off the bay.
   "That is your *Mayflower*," said Mr. Pipes, looking at the high
stern of the three-masted sailing vessel moored to the pier. A
seagull rose from a cluster of pilings near the ship and screeched
at them as it sailed overhead with the wind.
   "Humph!" retorted Dr. Dudley. "So that's it, is it?"
   "Boy, they sure have kept her up well over the years," said Annie, admiring the painted highlights running along the graceful
sheer of the little ship.
   "Wait a sec," said Drew. "That would make it at least 380
years old—do wooden ships last that long?"
   "No, indeed," said Mr. Pipes. "I say, this is *Mayflower II*, built
in Brixham, England, in 1955 and sailed in 1957 to Plymouth
in commemoration of the Pilgrim voyage in 1620. Lovely work."
   "What I wouldn't do to go sailing on a real ship like this one,"
said Drew.
   "Brixham?" said Annie, scowling in thought. "Brixham, that
sounds familiar."
   Drew scratched his head in thought. It did sound familiar.

"Wait, I've got it! 'Abide With Me'!" squealed Annie. "Didn't the man who wrote 'Abide With Me' live and preach at Brixham?"

"Yeah, it's a seaport town with lots of boats—Mr. Lyte!" said Drew. "That would be Henry Francis Lyte."

"Indeed," said Mr. Pipes with a smile, "how well you remember my little stories!"

"Well," said Dr. Dudley, brightening, "At any rate, it is a *British* ship. I thought she looked especially fine."

"Can we go on board?" asked Drew.

"Indeed," said Mr. Pipes. "That is precisely what we have come to do."

Their footsteps clomped along the wooden pier as they came near the ship. Drew studied the cold gray water of the harbor. Maybe it was so cold that fish didn't dare jump for fear of freezing, but he wondered....

"I can read your thoughts, my boy," said Mr. Pipes, putting his arm companionably around Drew's shoulders. "It's fishing that occupies your head, isn't it?"

"D'ya think we could?" said Drew, hopefully.

"Winter fishing in New England, I fear, can be rather hard," said Mr. Pipes.

"Impossible," corrected Dr. Dudley.

"Fishing will most likely have to wait until another time," said Mr. Pipes, consolingly.

"Yeah," said Drew.

"Now that's a nice touch," said Annie, looking at the high stern. "Somebody carved a pretty flower up there. What kind is it?"

"Let me guess," said Drew, rolling his eyes. "A *May* flower? What do you think? *May*, like springtime flowers. That reminds me of a joke: If April showers bring May flowers, what do *Mayflowers* bring?"

"What might they bring, my boy?" said Mr. Pipes, looking over his glasses at Drew.

"Pilgrims!" said Drew, laughing and slapping his thigh.

Dr. Dudley looked blankly at Drew as, this time, Annie rolled her eyes.

"Yes, well," said Mr. Pipes. "Back to your very good question, Annie. It is the hawthorn, or trailing arbutus, sometimes called the mayflower, thus the name of the vessel."

"Well, I think it is a pretty flower and a pretty ship with the same name," said Annie, with a toss of her head.

"The mayflower happens to be Massachusetts' state flower," said Mr. Pipes, leading them up the gangway.

"That makes a lot of sense," said Annie. Then she frowned and added, "But you're English; how do you know all this?"

Mr. Pipes smiled and said simply, "Books."

"It's big compared to *Toplady*," said Drew, "but not so big when you think about sailing across the Atlantic Ocean—way back then."

"How long do you estimate it to be, my boy?" asked Mr. Pipes.

"Hmm, a bit longer than a basketball court, I'd say."

"I'm not so very familiar with basketball courts," said Mr. Pipes, "but the *Mayflower II* is $106\frac{1}{2}$ feet, stem to stern, believed by historians to be very nearly the size and configuration of an ordinary merchant vessel of the 1620s."

Dr. Dudley had dropped behind and didn't seem to be listening. As they neared the level of the deck, and with a puzzled look on his face, he kept mumbling, "April showers … May flowers … hmm.…"

After paying their entrance fees and receiving their paper guide to the ship from the attendant, they strode around the deck of *Mayflower II*. Drew stood gazing up at the dizzying maze of tarred ropes and pulleys.

"Wow!" he said. "Take a look at this rope ladder! I could climb all the way up to that little round bathtub way up the mast. And here I go."

"Hey kid," said the attendant. "Just what does ya tink you's is doing, huh? Them's off limits t'da general pooblic, ya hears?"

Dr. Dudley scratched savagely at his ear and stared hard at the young man before turning away and muttering, "Shocking use of the language—if it is the same language, which I sincerely doubt."

"Yes, Drew," said Mr. Pipes, helping him off the rope ladder, "as fun as that might look, ratlines can be dangerous for the inexperienced. I say, let's go have a look at the cannons."

"But how am I going to get experienced?" moaned Drew, looking disappointed. "But *cannons*, did you say?" he added, following Mr. Pipes.

"Yes, but first we shall view the roundhouse," said Mr. Pipes, leading nimbly up a ladder to the half deck. "From just here," he paused, turning forward, taking in the strategic view of decks and rigging, "the conning officer, with perspective glass in hand, would direct the helmsman just below us on where to steer the ship." With a flush to his cheek and a faraway brightness in his eye, he added, "Lovely view of everything from the half deck of a merchant ship in those days."

"Wouldn't it be great to actually go sailing on this baby!" said Drew, looking up at the yards and imagining them creaking and groaning with billowing sails straining every thread and the deck beneath his feet heaving with the swell. He could just see himself—feet apart, arms akimbo, barking orders to his crew, and sailing into uncharted seas and exploring unknown lands and claiming them for....

"Drew, my boy," called Mr. Pipes, interrupting his reverie. "Do follow."

"Oh, oh, yeah, I-I'm coming," said Drew, with a glance over his shoulder. "You don't think they might just let us take her for—?"

"Impossible!" barked Dr. Dudley. "This is about as close to sailing as I care to get, thank you very much indeed!"

As they stepped into the roundhouse surrounded by heavy, well-oiled beams and planking, Annie breathed in the scent of linseed oil and felt the warmth of a big brass lantern suspended above a polished table fixed to the floor in the center of the room. Across the room Drew spied a cabinet full of muskets and pistols.

"Whoa! Check this out," he said, plastering his face against the steel grating of the cabinet doors. "Pirate pistols! Lots of them."

"Important place is a ship's roundhouse," said Mr. Pipes. "The first mate slept here, and it served as a chart room where officers plotted and planned the navigation of the ship."

"Why the guns?" asked Drew, turning—the impression of the metal grating crisscrossing his face comically.

"Well, you see," said Mr. Pipes, smiling, "the Great Cabin, where the commander of the original *Mayflower* lived, lies just below us, so if the crew ever mutinied—took over the ship, that is—then the roundhouse became a sort of fortress, well-armed to defend the officers against unruly seamen. Nothing of the sort happened in 1620, but mutiny happened often on board ships in those days—best to be prepared."

Annie put her elbows on the thick planks of the chart table. On the stiff yellow paper of an old map she admired the drawing of a ship, its sails taut with wind, and a sea monster spouting nearby.

"So the Mate used this map to get the Pilgrims from England to Plymouth?" she asked.

"Firstly, my dear," said Mr. Pipes, joined by the others around the chart table, "just as there are no 'ropes' on board a ship, there are no 'maps' either. 'Charts' one must call these navigational maps when on a ship."

"This chart, then?" Annie corrected herself.

"Well, you see," began Mr. Pipes, "that is precisely the trouble with the Pilgrims' voyage to Plymouth; they never intended to come here in the first place."

"Should have stayed in England," said Dr. Dudley with a sniff.

"Ah, but that was not an option we English gave Separatist Christians in those days," said Mr. Pipes. "Our Anglican archbishop Laud, more than any other, drove some of our greatest minds and godliest Christians from the realm. The Pilgrims fled to America because they wanted a pure church; they wanted to teach their children to worship God without James I or Laud forcing them to practice their faith the king's way for the king's political ends."

"Humph," grunted Dr. Dudley, "cannot see as that is a reason good enough."

"'Tis the best of all reasons for leaving the comforts and conveniences of England for this wilderness," responded Mr. Pipes.

"I'd agree that it is a wilderness," said Dr. Dudley, smugly.

"Let me explain," said Mr. Pipes. "The Pilgrims had secured a land grant from the Virginia Company and intended to join the thirteen-year-old Jamestown colony, but contrary winds blew them here, outside the jurisdiction of Virginia." He pointed to the coastline on the old chart. "Annie and Drew, do you remember the Reformation wall in Geneva where we read from your Mayflower Compact?"

"Yes," said Annie. "It was almost the only thing written in English."

"A most defining document in your history of self-government," said Mr. Pipes. "Those wise Christians knew that, as sinners, they must not leave the *Mayflower* before establishing a civil government and committing themselves to the rule of God's Law in political matters. Then, on the shores of that hostile wilderness—"

"Very little has changed" sniffed Dr. Dudley, with a glance out a porthole.

"Ahem." continued Mr. Pipes, his eyebrows bristling as he narrowed his eyes at his friend. "I say, on the shore, they fell to their knees and blessed God for His care of them on the perilous voyage. Hard times lay ahead that first winter—many died. But God remained with them; and, under the leadership of the saintly William Bradford their governor, they enjoyed a bountiful harvest that first year and feasted in celebration with the local Indians."

"That was our first Thanksgiving," said Annie.

"Never forget the object of that thanksgiving," said Mr. Pipes. "Many today have forgotten, I fear. Those first ill-equipped Pilgrims lit a candle, as it were, that shone as a beacon to all who would seek freedom on American shores. Oh, that all would render thanksgiving to God for that freedom."

On the chart, Drew traced the rocky hook of Cape Cod with his finger following the coastline north past Plymouth to Massachusetts Bay and Boston Harbor.

"So how did all the rest of Massachusetts get settled?" he asked.

"Well, things went from bad to worse when Charles I came to the throne of England in March of 1625. Greater persecution fell upon the Puritans—those followers of God's Word, as championed by the Reformation and John Calvin. Finally, in 1630, aboard seventeen ships came a large and well-funded group of godly Puritans to establish the Massachusetts Bay Colony. Well-organized and capable, these Christians came to build a 'wilderness Zion,' a commonwealth where the Bible would inform and guide both the state and the church. Governor John Winthrop, trained as a minister at Cambridge University in England, preached his famous sermon on board the *Arbella*. He consecrated the colony to be a model of Christian charity, where Christians would live, work, and worship—knit together by 'brotherly affection,' with the chief end of taking the gospel to the 'heathen.' The colony, built as a 'city upon a hill,' would be seen by all, if they were to 'deal falsely' with their God. Over the next ten years, 50,000 men, women, and children fled England—an England now on the eve of Civil War.

"Eighteen months after the first wave of this Great Migration, in 1631, on board the *Lyon* arrived a young man named John Eliot. Reared in a godly home in England and trained in languages and theology at Jesus College, Cambridge—for the Christian ministry—John would live out the ideals of the colony, perhaps more fully than anyone ever did. A man of great humility with a passion for souls, John was the most extraordinary man of this highly capable and well-educated colony.

"He eventually became the pastor of a new congregation in Roxbury near Boston, made up largely of immigrants from Nazeing, his hometown in Essex, England.

One year into his ministry, he recorded in the church register—with his own hand—his marriage to Hannah Eliot, the first marriage in Roxbury. For more than fifty years he 'loved, prized, and cherished' his dear wife who bore him six children of the covenant."

"Tell us more about his family," said Annie.

"Ah, yes, his family," said Mr. Pipes, a faraway sparkle to his eyes. "It was said that his home was a 'school of piety' and a 'Bethel for the worship of God.' He loved his wife and children dearly and blended tenderness with his desire that all in his house 'should keep the way of the Lord.' The Eliot home was crowned by daily family prayers, the reading of Scripture, and the singing of Psalms followed by the careful questioning of his dear ones to 'mend any error' in their understanding."

Annie glanced at Drew. This was so unlike their home, but it did remind her of their visit two summers ago to the godly British home of Bentley and Clara Howard, with all the sheep and lambs. What she wouldn't do to see her mother and stepfather come to know the Lord!

Mr. Pipes continued. "Mr. Eliot remembered well how, as a boy, family life and worship were the means of his 'owning the covenant' by a living faith. He described it like this: '… here the Lord said to my dead soul, live! live! and through the grace of God I do live and shall live forever!'"

Drew thought of Monsieur and Madame Charrue, whom they had also visited last summer in Switzerland. Mr. Eliot's family must have been like the Charrues, he decided, only speaking English instead of French.

Annie stared unseeingly at the old chart. She so wanted her mother and stepfather to know God's grace and live eternally. Surely, celebrating Christmas with Mr. Pipes would bring them to see their need of Jesus.

"As a preacher," Mr. Pipes went on, "Mr. Eliot determined to know nothing but Jesus Christ. He fed his lambs 'food not froth' in the Calvinist Puritan way with occasional 'flashes of lightening.'" Another Puritan minister, Cotton Mather, said of Eliot's preaching, '*Quot verba tot fulmina.*'"

"Huh?" said Drew.

Mr. Pipes laughed. "That's from the Latin and means that Mr. Eliot used thunderbolts as words, but he seasoned those words with grace and gentleness. And, of course, as in his home, he led his congregation in singing Psalms."

"Did he write some of them?" asked Annie. "I mean, versify some of them?"

"Ah, a fine question, Annie, my dear. The American Puritans, ever biblical, wanted to make a Psalter that was even more true to the original Hebrew poetry of the Psalms. Though still a young man, Eliot (and several others) was chosen by the colonial ministers to translate from the original Hebrew a versification of the Psalms suitable for public worship."

"So he spoke Hebrew?" said Drew.

"He was fluent in several languages, including Hebrew and Greek."

"Still, it must have been quite a job," said Annie. "There are 150 Psalms."

"Indeed," said Mr. Pipes. "Their goal was painstaking loyalty to the original text with less concern for poetic beauty than Sternhold and Hopkins, the standard Psalter of the day used by the Anglican Church. After several years of work, in 1640, the Bay Psalm Book became the first book printed in the American Colonies."

"That's really something!" said Annie. "Singing in worship must have been important to our Puritan forefathers."

"Yes, I think so," said Mr. Pipes.

"'Bay' in Bay Psalm Book," said Drew, pointing at the chart, "meant Massachusetts Bay, right?"

"Right you are," said Mr. Pipes. "During the work of translation, he kept up on all his family and pastoral duties—including traveling the surrounding countryside, visiting the sick and admonishing the wayward."

"Busy guy," said Drew. "Did he go fishing?"

"I really don't know," laughed Mr. Pipes. "Roxbury is right near the Old Harbor; and, for all I know, he may have taken his boys fishing on occasion. But he was particularly concerned about schooling in the colony. Sometime before 1645, Mr. Eliot founded the Roxbury Latin School with Philip Eliot, his brother, appointed first master of the school. Many historians insist Eliot's school is the oldest school in America."

"That's a lot for one guy to do in his lifetime," said Drew.

"Oh, you've only heard the beginning. After the Puritans became involved in an intertribal war with the Indians, called the Pequot War, Mr. Eliot started learning the Algonquin language from some of the local Indians."

"Wow! A real Indian war?" asked Drew, dancing around the chart table holding the fingers of one hand above his head like feathers while beating on his mouth with the other hand.

"Remember, war is not so glamorous as you imagine," said Mr. Pipes. "Eliot daily saw Indians on the streets of Roxbury come to trade with the white man, and soon the words of the original colonial charter rang clearly in his mind: '… to win the natives to the knowledge and obedience of the only true God and Savior.' Eliot, who it was said 'lived in heaven while he tarried on earth,' developed a deep longing for the salvation of his Indian neighbors. When he'd learned enough of the Algonquin language, he gathered Indians around him by giving them gifts, and then he taught them of the power and greatness of God Who made and rules the world and all things. He showed them how God's power and nature are seen in creation. Then he taught them God's Law, summarized in the Ten Commandments, and explained to them what punishment God had in store for all who break His Law. He then pointed them to Christ Jesus, the One Who gave his life to pay the punishment sinners deserve; and he urged them to offer up prayers of repentance and to trust in Christ alone for salvation. After each lesson, he encouraged the

Indians to ask questions so he could correct their misunderstandings."

"Just like in his family worship," said Annie, "with his kids."

"Exactly," said Mr. Pipes.

"What kinds of questions did they ask?" asked Drew.

"One Indian asked how God could hear Indians praying in Algonquin when he was used to hearing English prayers."

"Good question!" said Drew. "What did Mr. Eliot say?"

"He always answered with wisdom and consideration of their limitations in understanding. He told them that just as an Indian knows the different kinds of straw that he uses to make a basket, so God the Maker of all people knows and understands all his creatures regardless of language."

"Good answer," said Drew.

"Yes, but John Eliot was troubled by the question. These Indians did not have *one* page of God's Word in their own language; withal, even if they did, they had little use for the Bible, for none of them could read."

"He's pretty busy already," said Annie warily.

"Yes, but he longed for the Indians to know the living God Who speaks through His Word—the Bible, but only to those who understand its words. While some ministers debated whether they should bother evangelizing the Indians, Eliot went to work. He set about to create a written language from the Algonquin tongue, compiled a grammar book—so he could teach them their own language in written form, set up schools for the Indians, and began the enormous task of translating the entire Bible into this strange new language."

"What was so strange about it?" asked Annie.

"Well, Eliot wanted to teach them to pray, remember; and the phrase from Scripture, 'kneeling down to Him,' could be expressed in written form only by using thirty-four letters! Here, it looked like this." Mr. Pipes wrote on the edge of his *Mayflower II* guide, *Wutappesittukqussunnoohwehtunkquoh.*

"No kidding!" said Drew. "So all the words looked sort of like that?"

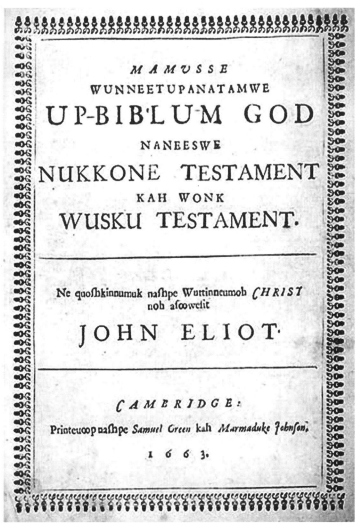

MAMVSSE

WUNNEETUPANATAMWE

UP-BIBLUM GOD

NANEESWE

NUKKONE TESTAMENT

KAH WONK

WUSKU TESTAMENT·

Ne quoſhkinnumuk naſhpe Wuttinncumoh *CHRIST*
noh aſoowelit

JOHN ELIOT·

CAMBRIDGE:

Printeuoop naſhpe *Samuel Green* kah *Marmaduke Johnſon,*

1 6 6 3.

"Yes," said Mr. Pipes. "The Indians asked Mr. Eliot many questions, and the Algonquin word for our word 'question' required forty-one letters to duplicate the Indians' sounds!"

"Easy solution," said Dr. Dudley. "Teach the savages English—the Queen's English, if you please—and all would be well."

"Not so simple as all that, my friend," said Mr. Pipes. "Many thought a man of Eliot's learning and genius could better expend his gifts and toil to more noble ends. Eliot never thought that way. It was an enormous task requiring great love and devotion both to God and to those benighted creatures—Eliot toiled faithfully for the glory of God, and God richly blessed his labors. Thousands of Indians began praying for forgiveness and God poured out His Spirit on thousands of Indians who became followers of Christ. Eliot trained Indian pastors in the 'art of teaching,' ordained elders and native pastors— John Hiacomes was the first American Indian pastor—and established schools for Indian children. John Eliot's Indians came to be called 'Praying Indians,' and great changes took place in their villages because of their prayers and Eliot's. Many of the 'Praying Villages' made their own laws against old practices like wife beating—"

"*Wife beating?*" interrupted Annie, her eyes wide.

"Ah, my dear, history relentlessly proves that every culture untouched by the sweet grace of the Christian Gospel practices horrible treatment of women," explained Mr. Pipes. "Algonquin Indians were no exception. They kept many wives, stole, and cheated, but the Christian Indians made their own laws against all this. They even made new laws about cleanliness; one such rule now declared it bad manners to kill head lice between your teeth!"

"Yuk!" said Annie. "The Indians actually used to do that?"

"So I am told," said Mr. Pipes. "But all things are made new by God's truth. The Christian Gospel affects all of life and culture. Finally, Mr. Eliot wanted his beloved Indians to sing in their worship services. So, in 1663, when he completed the final edition of the Old and New Testament, he included a versification of the Psalms in an Algonquin Psalter. His Indians were now praying and singing Indians!"

"He had to make Algonquin rhyme?" said Annie. "With all those sounds?"

"Indeed," said Mr. Pipes.

Drew frowned. "But wouldn't it be better for Indians to have their own Indian worship songs? I mean, after all, they were *Indians*, not Americans or English people. Besides, how could Indians, you know, *relate* to a Psalter?"

"Drew, my boy," said Mr. Pipes, looking over his glasses. "God gave us—all people—the Psalms with which to worship Him in song. And remember, He gave it to us in the Hebrew language, not in English *or* Algonquin. You might just as well ask why Americans should not have their own worship songs instead of God's. No, no, the Christian Church is united in her singing of Psalms and hymns to God, regardless of race or any other distinction."

"Still, it must have been really hard work making an Algonquin Psalter," said Annie.

"The difficulty of a task never seemed to daunt Mr. Eliot," replied Mr. Pipes. "He once wrote that 'prayers and pains through Christ Jesus will do anything.'"

Mr. Pipes paused and wrote ELIOT on his ship guidebook. Then, turning it, he held it up to the shiny brass lantern and said, "What does it say now?"

Drew squinted at the letters distorted by the curve of the brass lantern, but illuminated by its warm glow. "'TOILE.' What's that mean?"

"Wait, I think I know," said Annie. "They didn't spell things back then quite the way we do now. I'll bet they spelled 'toil,' you know, 'work,' with an *e* at the end. Mr. Eliot's name backward spells *toile!*"

"Fitting anagram for a man who lived eighty-six years, during which time he toiled ceaselessly for God's Kingdom. In his old age, those around him said he gained even more of the scent of heaven. His dear wife, Hannah, preceded him to the heavenly country where he longed to go, as well. Thinking his home going might be soon, he found an able replacement for his ministry at the Roxbury congregation. But he lived on and found himself still able to work—to toil—and he longed to be about his Father's business.

"Having long grieved over the condition of slaves in the colony, the venerable Eliot, with a 'bleeding and burning passion,' sent word to the surrounding slaveholders to send their poor black slaves to him for weekly spiritual instruction. Eliot, the 'model of Christian charity' himself, spent his last days teaching the outcasts of society of sin and grace and the wonderful freedom found in Christ. And more than any other individual, Mr. Eliot, 'the Apostle to the Indians,' brought Christian singing to *all* Americans—Indians included."

They left the roundhouse and followed Mr. Pipes through the ''tween decks,' where the Pilgrims and the chickens and pigs lived for the two stormy months during their pilgrimage to America.

"How about those cannons?" said Drew.

They moved aft, or back toward the stern, into the gun room where Mr. Pipes showed Drew the two "stern chasers"[†] mounted on either side of the large rudder near the waterline.

"The *Mayflower* was not equipped for pitched battle," said Mr. Pipes. "But her crew would try to outrun any would-be pirates while firing these minions straight aft at her pursuers. Pretty effective up to 2,500 yards."

"That'll teach 'em not to tailgate!" said Drew.

◈ ◈ ◈

After descending the gangway and while walking along the pier, Drew looked back at *Mayflower II* and almost stumbled on the planking. Dr. Dudley, muttering softly, brought up the rear.

Suddenly he burst out laughing. "Yes, yes, it is perfectly clear. April showers bring May flowers. What do *Mayflowers* bring? Ha, ha! Yes, yes, you meant the ship—*Mayflower*, the ship!" He doubled over with laughter and nearly fell off the pier into the icy water. "*Mayflowers* bring Pilgrims! Yes, yes, of course. Oh, well-told joke, Drew, my boy—jolly well-told, indeed!"

---

† A term coined in the early nineteenth century for guns mounted at the rear of a sailing ship and pointing back off the stern.

Chapter Three

Samuel Davies
1723-1761

Great God of wonders! all Thy ways
    Are worthy of Thyself divine;
And the bright glories of Thy grace
    Among Thine other wonders shine:
Who is a pard'ning God like Thee?
Or who has grace so rich and free?

That afternoon, after returning the car to the rental office, the foursome boarded a Greyhound bus for Princeton, New Jersey.

Sitting next to Mr. Pipes, Annie gazed out the window, biting her pencil. It looked bleak and cold with globs and splotches of old dirty snow littering the edges of the highway. "How do you draw *that*?" she mused. Annie decided that maybe it was poetry weather; now what would be a good first line....

"There's not much green around here this time of year," she said at last. "It's all gray and even the trees look cold—but I'll bet it's pretty when it snows—everything all cozy in a fluffy white blanket. Do you think it will snow?" she concluded, to no one in particular.

Dr. Dudley, sitting next to Drew in front of them, turned, "I have little knowledge of American weather patterns; and besides, what I think about it doesn't much matter, now does it? If it is to snow, it jolly well will do it, without my thinking about it."

He turned and, with a rustle and snap, resumed reading the *New York Times*. Annie was afraid Dr. Dudley's feelings were hurt by how eagerly everyone had chimed in, supporting Mr. Pipes's suggestion that Dr. Dudley might be too weary to drive to Princeton, especially on unfamiliar roads in winter weather.

"I hadn't thought of it that way," she replied, trying to sound sweet.

Mr. Pipes leaned toward the window and stared hard at the thin gray clouds.

"Well, now, my dear," he began with a smile, "I predict the weather by several factors: the most reliable of which is my aging joints; rarely do they deceive me in this."

"So what do your 'aging joints' think?" asked Drew, turning eagerly.

"Joints can't *think*," said Dr. Dudley. "I know; I am a doctor."

"True," said Mr. Pipes, "but they can creak and groan a bit now and then."

Annie looked at their old friend with concern.

"I'll route the bus to the nearest hospital," said Dr. Dudley, turning in alarm, then reaching for his leather doctor's bag. "It will only take a jiffy. Do stay calm."

"Don't be utterly ridiculous," laughed Mr. Pipes, with a wave of his hand. "When one approaches John Eliot's age, creaks and groans are as normal as—" he smiled at Drew, "—as normal as hunger pangs are for you, my dear boy. No, you see, my joints are telling me—in a manner of speaking—that we will likely have snow soon."

"How soon?" asked Annie.

"That is where it gets slightly less clear, my dear," said Mr. Pipes. "But I still maintain that it will snow—soon."

"Oh, I love snow," said Annie, scrunching her shoulders in anticipation. Then a thought occurred to her. "B-but it won't snow so hard we can't get home, will it?" It would be terrible if her parents didn't get to know Mr. Pipes better; she had hoped and prayed for months that he would help bring them to salvation.

"Not at all likely, my dear," said Mr. Pipes.

"But with our luck," said Drew, "it'll snow just after we leave for home; we've only got four days, you know—three and a half, now."

"Drew, my dear fellow," said Mr. Pipes. "You must be grateful: four whole days and nights with so much to see and enjoy together. The glass is, to be sure, four days *full*—not empty."

❖ ❖ ❖

Several hours later the bus arrived in Princeton, and after eating at one of Drew's favorite fast-food restaurants—Mr. Pipes cutting each bite of his hamburger with a plastic fork and knife—they checked into a bed and breakfast near Princeton University and collapsed into bed, exhausted from their travels.

Next morning, Drew polished off three plates of Belgian waffles topped with maple syrup and five or six sausages—he lost count. Annie passed on the sausages. They all shared a pot of tea that Dr. Dudley said was "tolerable (sniff) for *American* brewing." After packing their things and bundling up against the New Jersey cold, they walked down Witherspoon Street to Nassau Street where they had gotten off the bus last night. They passed through the commanding FitzRandolph Gateway into the palatial campus of Princeton University.

"Now that looks pretty old for America," said Drew, rubbing his hands together and blowing on them as an imposing sandstone building came into view through the leafless branches of oak trees. "What's so important about this place?" he added.

"Ah, yes, well Nassau Hall," began Mr. Pipes.

"NASA?" Drew cut him off. "You mean this is NASA, where they make spaceships to send to Mars? I thought it would look more modern."

"No, no, my boy," laughed Mr. Pipes, "Nassau Hall, named in honor of the Protestant king of England, William III of Orange-Nassau. In 1756, Nassau Hall housed the entire university," said Mr. Pipes. "They considered naming it after the governor of New Jersey, but ..."

"Why didn't they?" asked Annie. "At least he must have been an American."

"Tut, tut, my dear, naming even an American institute of higher—" began Dr. Dudley, "I say, naming an American *school* after a British monarch shows some considerable taste, I should think. Perhaps there's hope after all."

"Oh, indeed, naming this hall after the king was the superior choice, I assure you. For, you see," said Mr. Pipes, his eyebrows rumpled in a frown, "if my memory serves, the governor's name was—something Belcher."

"Belcher?" laughed Drew, "that would be a good one!"

"Ahem, perhaps not," said Mr. Pipes. "In its day, Nassau Hall was the largest academic building in the western hemisphere. And during your war for independence—"

"Call it what it was," Dr. Dudley cut him off, "a *revolution*, a defiance of king and country. Humph!"

"Yes, well," Mr. Pipes continued, "nevertheless, Nassau Hall played a very important role."

"No kidding?" said Drew, as they came alongside the massive walls and round-arched windows.

Dr. Dudley frowned up at the building.

Mr. Pipes continued, "Troops from both the American colonial army and the British used it for a garrison and hospital; and, in 1777, at the Battle of Princeton, some British soldiers fleeing George Washington's troops took cover inside her twenty-six-inch thick walls. They chopped up the pews for firewood—"

"No doubt it was very cold," said Dr. Dudley, glancing up at the menacing clouds.

"We British were finally driven from the hall," continued Mr. Pipes, "when colonial cannonballs shook the stout building. One cannonball, so goes the legend, crashed through the walls, decapitating a portrait of George II, former King of England."

"What a shot!" cried Drew, slapping his fist into his palm.

"Balderdash!" snorted Dr. Dudley. "Pure legend born of wishful thinking."

"I hope the man in the painting was the only one who got hurt," said Annie.

"Oh, my dear, your liberty came at a great price," said Mr. Pipes. "Late in the war—1783, I believe it was—Nassau Hall actually housed the Continental Congress and briefly served as your nation's capitol. The Congress commissioned the celebrated artist and patriot soldier, Charles Willson Peale, to paint a battle portrait of George Washington. And, in something of a symbolic gesture, they placed in the frame of the beheaded king Washington's new portrait. It adorns these stout walls to this day."

"A desecration!" said Dr. Dudley.

"Hey, is that a real cannon sticking out of the grass over there?" asked Drew, pointing excitedly.

"It is," replied Mr. Pipes, "a cannon used at the Battle of Princeton during the Revolutionary War and later in the War of 1812."

"Kind of odd way of showing it off," said Drew as they rounded the corner of the building.

"Can we go inside?" asked Annie. "I'd love to see the painting, and I think it's going to rain."

"I believe we might be admitted, my dear," said Mr. Pipes. "The entrance lies just around the corner."

"Check out these tigers!" said Drew, stroking the laid-back ears of one of the bronze tigers guarding the entrance.

"Being from out west," continued Drew, rejoining Mr. Pipes on the stone steps of the hall, and gazing up at the round arch of the tall doorway "I never actually realized we had buildings as old as the revolution."

"Oh, this one is something older than the revolution," said Mr. Pipes, leading them across the large entryway into the Prayer Room. "And some of the greatest men have taught, preached, and studied in these walls; George Whitefield once preached a sermon here at 5 o'clock in the morning. You see, The College of New Jersey, as it was then called, received its charter in 1746, and Princeton was chosen as the permanent site of the college in 1752. But no other individual deserves as much credit for raising money to build this first building—and, for a time, the only building—as the young Presbyterian minister, Samuel Davies."

"Aha, Davies sounds Welsh to my ear," said Dr. Dudley, cocking his head to one side.

Annie gazed around the dark polished panels of the chapel. A warm glow came from the chandeliers hanging overhead, and cloudy gray light filtered through large windows flanked by fluted columns and crowned with intricately carved capitals. Oil paintings in gold-gilded frames hung around the room. Annie pulled her parka off and strolled around the chapel, gazing into the faces of pious Puritans and stern statesmen.

"Must be new pews," said Drew.

"Indeed," said Mr. Pipes.

"Who are these people?" asked Annie from across the room.

"Well, that one next to your American flag is—" began Mr. Pipes.

"George Washington!" Drew cut him off. "Hey, and this must be the painting that replaced the king's picture. I like Washington's sword."

"Yes, and over there next to our flag, the Union Jack, you will find King William of Orange," said Mr. Pipes.

"Handsome fellow, indeed," said Dr. Dudley.

"And just there," Mr. Pipes pointed at a portrait of a man with a wig and ruffled collar, "is James Madison, former student of Princeton and the father of your Constitution. The rest would be founders, early presidents and alumni of the college," continued Mr. Pipes.

"Which one is Mr. Davies?" asked Annie.

"Well, there is Jonathan Edwards," replied Mr. Pipes, pointing at a wigged portrait, "perhaps, the greatest American theologian and thinker, and the third president of Princeton. And just to the right is Samuel Davies."

"Even with that white wig," said Annie, gazing at his peaceful features, framed by powdered curls, "he looks pretty young."

"How did he go about raising the money for this place?" asked Drew.

"American colonials certainly would not have had the means," said Dr. Dudley, under his breath.

"Good question, Drew, but allow me to pick up the story somewhat earlier," said Mr. Pipes, settling into a well-polished pew and crossing his legs, his hands clasped around his knee.

"Dr. Dudley, you are correct, Davies is of Welsh extraction, but more importantly, his parents were ardent Christians—loyalty to Christ must always come before loyalty to one's country. In later years, he referred to himself as 'a son of prayer,' for his mother especially asked the Lord for him."

"Like Hannah in the Bible," said Annie.

"Hey, and like Hannah's boy," said Drew, "his name is Samuel, too."

"Precisely," said Mr. Pipes. "At an early age, Samuel showed a lively tenderness towards the things of God and soon became and continued to be throughout his life the most unsparing judge of his life as a Christian. His parents placed him under the tutelage of the saintly Mr. Blair at his 'log college' across the Delaware River in Pennsylvania. Blair trained some of the most important Christian leaders America ever produced; Davies later described Blair's log college as 'the gate of heaven.' And then, at only twenty-three years of age he began his life as a Presbyterian evangelist, receiving the first license to preach as a dissenting minister in predominantly Anglican Virginia. In 1746, he married and after some months began his missionary work in the backwoods. Some time later, feverish and sick from overwork, he rode home on horseback one hundred miles only to find his wife struggling for her life and the life of their son soon to be born. She and the child died only days later."

"That's so sad," said Annie.

"Yes, yes it is," said Mr. Pipes, gazing out one of the tall windows into the gray distance before continuing. "After some months of grief and ill health, Mr. Davies answered a call to be pastor of the Presbyterian Church in Hanover, Virginia. Davies continued to travel, preaching at different meeting houses that did not have their own minister. Eventually he served seven congregations, travelling up to 500 miles in two months and preaching upwards of forty sermons in his travels, all in poor health."

"That's a lot of work!" said Drew.

"He must have been worn out all the time," said Annie.

"Yes, it was a great deal of work, but with the excellent help and encouragement of his second wife, Jane Holt, his health for a time improved and he found great pleasure in his ministry. But, more lay in store for this young preacher. God's Spirit moved in response to Davies' prayers and faithful preaching. Many nominal Anglicans in Virginia were converted under his preaching; moreover, men and women—both high and low, gentleman and slave—came to living faith in the Lord Jesus. Davies wrote 'I am as happy as perhaps creation can make me. I have a peaceful study, the venerable dead are waiting in my library to entertain me. I very much question if there is a more calm, placid, and contented mortal in Virginia.'"

"The 'venerable dead?'" said Annie, wrinkling her nose. "What on earth does that mean?"

"Books, my dear, books," said Mr. Pipes. "Books written by men long dead but who still speak—even today. Books like ones written by Richard Baxter, who described the reformed pastor as one 'to preach as never sure to preach again, and as a dying man to dying men.' There is perhaps no better description of Samuel Davies himself than in those words.

"His congregations grew with wealthy gentlemen and their black slaves praying, singing Psalms and hymns, and hearing the preaching of God's Word together in one place. In Davies' assemblies, the broken bread and wine of the Lord's supper was received equally by black hand and white. One man described being among the devout worshipers in Davies's care as like residing in 'the suburbs of heaven.' Education spread and a whole generation of black slaves grew up learning to read under Davies's pious influence; Davies asked wealthier Christians to supply good books which the black Christians received with 'passionate gratitude.' One book much loved was Isaac Watts' *Psalms of David Imitated*, first published in America in 1729, by Benjamin Franklin. George Whitefield used Watts in his evangelistic preaching around the colonies, and so did Samuel Davies, giving away many copies of Watts to Christians in his wide parish."

"I guess Isaac Watts would be one of the 'venerable dead,'" said Drew.

"Indeed," said Mr. Pipes. "Davies loved poetry and wrote in verse himself. He no doubt would have included all the great hymn writers in that designation."

"I love Watts's poetry," said Annie.

"Remember that John Wesley also loved Watts's hymns and published the first Anglican hymnal, including many Watts hymns, and John's translation of German ones, in Georgia in 1737. This got him a bit, shall we say, in the soup with Anglican authorities.

"Mr. Davies's converts also loved Watts," continued Mr. Pipes. "He describes how his own kitchen would be filled with black Christians who loved worshipping God with Psalms and hymns at any time of the day or night. He wrote, 'Sometimes when I waked about two or three o'clock in the morning, a torrent of sacred harmony poured into my chamber and carried me away to heaven.'"

"I would love to hear that," said Annie, a faraway look in her eyes.

"One's sleep, however, would be somewhat disturbed," said Dr. Dudley.

"Davies's part in this revival of true faith was interrupted when the Presbyterian Synod of New York, with the encouragement of George Whitefield, urged him to join Gilbert Tennent in a fund-raising voyage to England to raise support for the young college. American Presbyterians placed a high priority on the importance of an educated clergy; the purpose of Princeton would be training young men to carry on the work of the gospel in the growing congregations.

"Arriving in London December 25, 1753, Davies soon found English Presbyterianism to be cold and formal with definite objections to his Calvinism; Presbyterian pulpits were soon closed to him. Baptist Christians, however, received him with appreciation; but, as they placed less importance on an educated clergy, they offered little support for the college. George Whitefield and John and Charles Wesley, all Anglicans, offered the greatest support, from whom the original funds for this very building came."

"Aha," said Dr. Dudley, looking around the hall with new interest, "so this fine hall was built with English money—I knew there was something about it the moment I stepped in the door. Yes, yes, a fine piece of work, indeed."

They all laughed.

"While in England," continued Mr. Pipes, "Mr. Davies's preaching eventually came to the attention of the King, George II, and Davies was invited to preach at the royal chapel."

"We're talking the same George II whose picture got it with the cannon?" asked Drew, drawing his finger across his neck with a "Kkkik."

"Indeed," said Mr. Pipes. "And while twenty-nine-year-old Davies preached before his Majesty, the king frequently whispered with his advisors. Davies finally halted and said, 'When the lion roars, the beasts of the forest all tremble; and when King Jesus speaks, the princes of the earth should keep silence.'"

"The cheek!" spluttered Dr. Dudley.

"Way to go, Mr. Davies!" said Drew at the same time.

"What did he mean by King Jesus speaking?" asked Annie.

"Mr. Davies understood that the faithful preaching of the Word of God is the Word of God. Surprisingly, the king took no offense and explained that he was so astonished at the young preacher's giftedness he felt compelled to comment on it to his advisors; Davies finished his sermon before a silent king, whom he regarded highly all his days.

"As he should," sniffed Dr. Dudley.

"Davies returned to America, after a frightfully stormy voyage across the Atlantic. He resumed his preaching ministry in Hanover after a three-week wait in foul weather on board the little ship in Plymouth harbor and a long winter ride on horseback. With the money raised, they built Nassau Hall, and this chapel served as the center of Presbyterian worship in the area. The first organ used in American Presbyterian worship echoed from these very walls for many years.

"After the death of the president of the college—Aaron Burr, godly son-in-law of the celebrated revival preacher, Jonathan Edwards—Edwards himself became president of the college. He, too, died after only a short term of leadership. The trustees of the college turned to Davies, who first refused and then—only after considerable pressure—accepted the call. Davies, one of America's greatest preachers, served as president for eighteen months; his clear passionate preaching filled this very room many times during those months."

Drew looked at the pulpit and then at the portrait of Samuel Davies. What would it have been like, he wondered, to sit in this room and hear him preach?

"It is said that Davies preached his own funeral sermon right here," continued Mr. Pipes.

"What!" cried Annie.

"You see, his New Year's Day sermon, preached in 1761, came from the text in Jeremiah 28:16, 'This year thou shalt die.' He wanted to alarm careless and unconverted students as to the shortness of life; he told them that it was highly probable that death might meet some of them that very year. 'Perhaps I may die this year,' he said, as he urged them to repent and make good use of their lives, living each day of the coming year for Christ. One month later, Samuel Davies died, aged only thirty-seven years. His mother stood by his side as he fell asleep in Jesus. 'There is

the son of my prayers,' she said, 'but there is the will of God and
I am satisfied.' They conducted his funeral service here in the
Prayer Room."

Cold rain pattered against the tall windows as Mr. Pipes finished the story.

"Do you know any of Mr. Davies's poems?" asked Annie.
"You said he liked poetry."

"That I do," replied Mr. Pipes, rising to his feet. "But I propose bundling ourselves up and making our way to the University Chapel where I will teach you his greatest poem, worthy to
be ranked among the great hymns of Christian worship."

▩ ▩ ▩

A kindly woman in an office near the entrance of the Hall
loaned them two large umbrellas "to keep off the chill of the
freezing rain," she said. They thanked her and left behind Nassau
Hall, with its white domed spire rising into the steel gray drizzle.
Then they splashed their way past two much larger bronze tigers,
who, with bared teeth, looked ready to pounce.

"They look like real tigers—only bigger," said Drew, leaving
the orange and black striped umbrella—with the din of the rain
pelting it—to Dr. Dudley. With raindrops hitting his face, he
reached up and touched the enormous teeth of one of the tigers.
"These guys could do some damage," he said.

"Why tigers?" asked Annie, from the safety of her umbrella
shared with Mr. Pipes.

"Princeton mascot, I should think," offered Dr. Dudley.
"Hmm, one male and one female," he added, puzzled.

"Yes, yes, I did read something about tigers," said Mr. Pipes.
"These tigers marked the opening of the university to women,
making Princeton co-educational. Women were not accepted as
students until 1969, in part because of its original purpose of
training men for the Christian ministry—a mission from which
Princeton, sad to say, has strayed rather far."

"Hmm, tigers," said Annie, "that maybe accounts for the orange and black umbrellas, do you think?"

"Perhaps," said Mr. Pipes. "But we may have the proverbial cart before the horse."

"Wait!" said Drew, rejoining them as they walked on. "Wasn't Nassau Hall named for that king?"

"Yes, William of Orange-Nassau," said Mr. Pipes.

"Well, there it is, then," said Annie. "Orange for the prince of Orange, and tigers have orange stripes—and make good mascots."

"A scorned origin, I should think," said Dr. Dudley.

▧ ▧ ▧

As they walked across a broad courtyard paved with bricks shiny from the rain, the University Chapel loomed into view, framed by the black arms of leafless trees.

"One of the most beautiful Gothic buildings in America," said Mr. Pipes.

"*Neo*-Gothic, if you please," corrected Dr. Dudley.

"Whatever-Gothic, it's beautiful," said Annie.

"And it is one of the three largest college churches in the world," said Mr. Pipes, gazing up at the arches and buttresses of the grand building.

"English architect, no doubt," insisted Dr. Dudley.

"No, I think not," said Mr. Pipes. "An American fellow named Cram, lovely work indeed. He breathed new life into a style that remains ageless. Though students are home on holiday, I'm told the chapel is open until noon each day; let us escape the rain and have a look."

▧ ▧ ▧

Inside, a thrill came over Annie and Drew that they first experienced over a year and a half ago when they stumbled into the ancient parish church of St. Peter and St. Paul's in Mr. Pipes's village of Olney.

"What was the word, Mr. Pipes?" asked Drew in hushed tones, as he felt once again the wonder of the row-upon-row of columns and pointed arches and the multi-colored light muted by clouds but streaming in the stained-glass windows. "'Grandeur,' wasn't that it?"

"That's it," whispered Annie, walking down the central aisle of the nave.

The rest followed her toward the north window. Suddenly she heard a rustling of paper and the "thunk" of a book hitting the floor and echoing throughout the stone walls.

"I think someone might be here," she said in a whisper.

"Yeah," added Drew. "And there's a light up there."

And then a barrage of sound suddenly poured from rows of pipes forward of the nave. Mr. Pipes closed his eyes, winced now and then, and smiled.

"The organist is practicing," shouted Drew. "And it just fills up the whole place. Wow! He's really good!"

The music abruptly stopped as happens sometimes when someone is practicing, and Drew's final words boomed throughout the quiet chapel.

"Drew!" hissed Annie.

"Hey, thanks a lot," came a young voice from the console of the organ.

"We're really sorry to disturb your playing," said Annie, as they joined the organist.

"Hey, no sweat," the organist said, shrugging his shoulders and pushing up his glasses. Drew thought he looked like a college student with his orange-hooded sweatshirt and jeans; his deck shoes lay carelessly to one side. Drew looked at his bright orange socks and decided stocking feet probably helped playing the foot pedals better.

"Fact is, I'm glad for the interruption," the young man continued. "This place gets kind a' lonely—especially over winter break; almost everyone's gone home, you know."

"And why must you stay?" asked Mr. Pipes, kindly.

"Oh, you're a Brit, or something," said the organist, smiling and extending his hand in greeting.

"The children, however, are from your side of the pond," said Dr. Dudley. "My colleague and I are—Englishmen."

Drew thought he detected a bit more elaborate British accent than usual in Dr. Dudley's reply, but he couldn't be sure.

"Hi, I'm Joe," the young man said. Mr. Pipes introduced them. "I'm supposed to play this Bach cantata for a Christmas Eve service." Joe pushed his glasses up and ran his hand through his dark hair, holding on to a wad of it for a moment and pulling. "But, for the life of me, I can't seem to get this part right."

"Hey, we can help," said Drew.

Joe's eyes narrowed as he looked down at Drew's confident smile and said, "*You* can help *me?*"

Drew felt his cheeks getting hot. "Well, *I* can't, but Mr. Pipes can—he's a famous organist from *England.*"

"Not at all famous," corrected Mr. Pipes, moving closer and studying the music over the young organist's shoulder. "But I just may be able to offer some assistance."

"Here's the problem passage," said Joe pointing at several lines of music so thick with sixteenth notes that Drew thought it looked like an army of black ants climbing stairs.

"May I?" asked Mr. Pipes, gesturing toward the rows of keys.

"She's all yours," said Joe, moving aside, but looking a little skeptical.

Mr. Pipes adjusted his glasses, rubbed his hands together, breathed deeply and began playing.

As the strains rose effortlessly from keys to pipes and re-echoed through the lofty interior of the chapel, Joe looked from the old man's fingers to the music and then at Mr. Pipes's face—his eyes were closed!

With an unpretentious trill, the music ended.

"Bach does demand considerable concentration," remarked Mr. Pipes, breathing on his glasses and wiping them on his handkerchief. He resettled them on his nose and continued. "Perhaps you will need to slow the tempo."

Joe's mouth hung open as he looked at the old man. Drew crossed his arms and, with a smug grin at Joe, gave a sideways nod of his head toward Mr. Pipes, then said, "See, told ya."

"That was great!" said Joe, when he found his voice.

"This is a very fine instrument, indeed," said Mr. Pipes. "Who is its builder?"

"English chap, no doubt," mumbled Dr. Dudley. "Though *they* never admit such things."

"Oh, some guy out west—Paul Fritts—from a Podunk place near Tacoma—all timber and teepees out there," replied Joe. "But they do build great organs."

❖ ❖ ❖

For the next half-hour, Mr. Pipes worked with Joe on the difficult passage of Bach while Annie and Drew strolled around the chapel. They gazed together at the north window, the rain pattering against its colored panes.

"That must be Jesus," said Annie, "in the middle with the crown of thorns."

Drew felt overwhelmed by all the images until his eye found an angel holding an enormous broadsword and several knights clad in armor carrying swords and shields.

"Oh, Drew, look at the windows below Jesus; they're beating Him and nailing Him to the cross."

"I wonder if students and teachers at Princeton still believe in Him like Samuel Davies did," said Drew.

"They've got plenty to remind them of Him in this chapel," said Annie.

"Yeah, look at the words carved in the stone under the window," said Drew.

"'He that shall endure unto the end, the same shall be saved,'" read Annie. "I wonder if Princeton has?"

"Has what?"

"Endured," said Annie.

"It's still here, isn't it?" said Drew, looking back at the expanse of the nave.

"But 'endure unto the end' doesn't mean the buildings," said Annie. "It's talking about true faith in Jesus as Lord and Savior—I'm sure that's what it means."

◪ ◪ ◪

Soon the music stopped and the children joined Mr. Pipes and the rest at the organ.

"Ah, children," said Mr. Pipes, "Joe was just telling me something of the history of organs and of Princeton."

"He was telling *you*?" asked Drew. "So he knows about Nassau Hall and the first pipe organ in Presbyterian worship in America, like you told us?"

"I-I'd never heard that," said Joe.

"Maybe he knows about Samuel Davies's hymn," said Annie, "remember, the one you were going to teach us?"

"Now I do know that he was fourth president of Princeton," said Joe. "But I didn't know he wrote a hymn. Let's hear it."

Mr. Pipes consulted one of the hymnals in a nearby pew and, opening it, put it on the music stand above the keyboards. "Davies actually wrote sixteen hymns. And, like all great hymn writers, he found his inspiration in the Psalms. His love of Isaac Watts's poetry is also evident in the best of his hymns. His most loved hymn, either side of the pond—as you call it, Dr. Dudley—at one time appeared in more than one hundred English hymnals.…"

"Astonishing!" interrupted Dr. Dudley. "An American hymn writer appearing in British hymnals. Must have been his Welsh blood."

"Our friend, John Newton, who lived at the same time as Mr. Davies, composed the lovely tune 'Sovereignty' for Davies's best hymn, 'Great God of Wonders!' It goes like this," said Mr. Pipes. He played a simple melody, which changed tempo in the refrain. Drew liked the rising, almost marching sound of the last lines; he felt that surging in his blood that came when he sang "The Son of God Goes Forth to War."

"I love Mr. Newton's tune," said Annie. "Mr. Pipes is the organist at John Newton's church in England," she added to Joe, who scratched his head.

"Wasn't Newton the guy," he wondered to himself, "who long ago discovered gravity at Cambridge?" Obviously, he was thinking of Sir Isaac Newton, the great British physicist.

"But Mr. Newton was a *minister*, not a musician," said Drew. "How could he write such good music?"

"Remember, Drew, that knowing God's Word is the most important ingredient to writing great hymns," said Mr. Pipes. "And perhaps biblical and theological understanding are essential to writing great hymn tunes as well. In any case, Newton marshaled and cultivated all his gifts to holy ends, including any musical ability he possessed. You must do the same."

Joe cleared his throat awkwardly.

Annie grabbed another hymnal and turned to Davies's hymn. "Now that's a great first line," she thought, as she read the poetry.

> Great God of wonders! all Thy ways
> > Are worthy of Thyself divine;
> And the bright glories of Thy grace
> > Among Thine other wonders shine:
> Who is a pard'ning God like Thee?
> Or who has grace so rich and free?

"This hymn text is all about the wonder—" began Mr. Pipes.

Drew cut him off. "Wait! You said Mr. Davies liked Watts— I think I've got something here—and Isaac Watts's hymns are all about wonder, I remember you said that. Maybe that's why Davies starts his hymn with the God of *wonders*."

"You may very well have something, my boy," said Mr. Pipes. "Davies's hymn is all about wonder at the pardoning grace of God—grace so rich and free."

"And 'grace' was one of Mr. Newton's favorite words," added Annie, humming the first bars of "Amazing Grace."

"Because he understood the word, 'sin,'" concluded Mr. Pipes—with Drew and Annie chiming in on the word "sin."

Joe blinked several times and ran his fingers through his hair as Mr. Pipes pulled out the stops and played an introduction, Newton's melody rising to the Gothic vaulting high above.

> Pardon from an offended God!
> Pardon for sins of deepest dye!
> Pardon bestowed through Jesus' blood!
> Pardon that brings the rebel nigh!
>
> O may this glorious, matchless love,
> This God-like miracle of grace,
> Teach mortal tongues, like those above,
> To raise this song of lofty praise:
> Who is a pard'ning God like Thee?
> Or who has grace so rich and free?

Joe stared soberly at the hymnal.

"My dear young man," said Mr. Pipes, smiling kindly at Joe, "meditate on the words of this hymn, on your sins of deepest dye, on grace so rich and free, on God's pardon that brings the rebel nigh. Be that contrite rebel, find the pardon bestowed through Jesus' blood and raise to Jesus songs of lofty praise."

Great God of Wonders!

Who is a God like you, who pardons sin and forgives the transgression? Mic. 7:18

1. Great God of won - ders! All thy ways are match-less, god - like,
2. In won - der lost, with trem- bling joy we take the par - don
3. O may this strange, this match- less grace, this god - like mir - a -

and di - vine; but the fair glo - ries of thy grace more god - like
of our God; par - don for crimes of deep- est dye, a par - don
cle of love, fill the whole earth with grate-ful praise, and all th'an -

and un - ri - valed shine, more god- like and un - ri - valed shine.
bought with Je - sus' blood, a par - don bought with Je - sus' blood.
gel - ic choirs a - bove, and all th'an - gel - ic choirs a - bove.

REFRAIN

Who is a par - d'ning God like thee? Or who has grace so

rich and free? Or who has grace so rich and free?

Samuel Davies, 1723–1761
Alt. 1961

SOVEREIGNTY (or WONDERS) L.M.rep.ref.
John Newton, 1725–1807

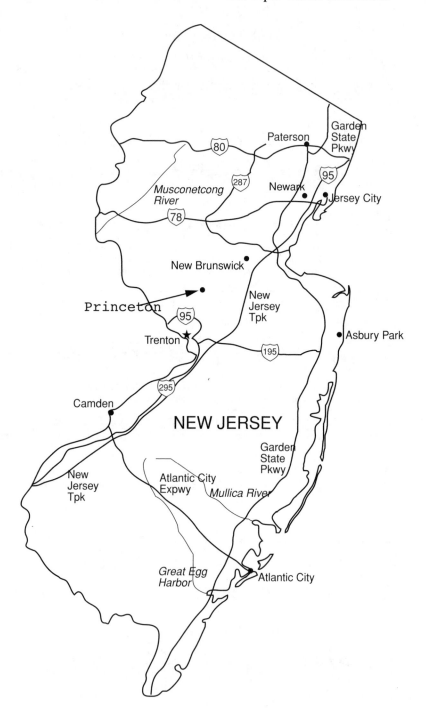

Chapter Four

Timothy Dwight
1752–1817

Beyond my highest joy
I prize her heav'nly ways,
Her sweet communion, solemn vows,
Her hymns of love and praise.

"You know, Mr. Pipes," said Drew, looking carefully at the old man's face as they left the chapel, "you're looking kinda—" he squinted into the old man's twinkling eyes, "well, kinda *hungry*."

"Indeed!" laughed Mr. Pipes.

"Yeah, and I'll bet your stomach's been growling for hours," added Drew with a grin. "It's an emergency, Dr. Dudley, we've got to get Mr. Pipes something to eat—and fast!"

"Oh, Drew," said Annie, shaking her head as she zipped up her coat.

"I say," said Dr. Dudley. "He simply must not dine at another of your American fast-food places, you know, like the one run by the fellow of Scots extraction who wears that awful clown suit. Humph! Food prepared fast and eaten fast has a most detrimental effect on one's digestion. Mr. Pipes, dear man, do you know of some place for our luncheon a bit more—well, *civilized*? If you do, I'll shout you all for luncheon. My treat."

"In fact I do," replied Mr. Pipes. "Hmm, the rain has all but stopped. Perhaps we might hail a cab and make our way the short distance to The Class of 1887 Boathouse on Lake Carnegie."

"A boathouse?" gasped Dr. Dudley. "You're not actually thinking of hiring one of those wretched things, are you? Why, man it's the dead of winter! And do I need to remind you that people—"

"Yes, yes, I am quite aware of your concerns," said Mr. Pipes, halting Dr. Dudley with a wave of his hand.

"A boathouse!" said Annie and Drew eagerly.

"I was thinking first of luncheon," said Mr. Pipes. "Princeton University has something of a history of crew—rowing, you know, very sleek fast boats. And they have a lovely old boathouse on a lake very nearby. Do let's go and see if we might dine there."

"Yes, let's!" said Annie and Drew.

"But, do promise they'll be no—no *boats* about?" stammered Dr. Dudley

"Oh, I can promise no such thing," said Mr. Pipes.

❖ ❖ ❖

Moments later the yellow taxicab turned off Washington Road and deposited them in front of The Boathouse. Annie admired the rows of Gothic arches on the main level of the white stucco building. And Drew scanned the gray water of the lake for boats.

"It does look kind of cold for boating out there," Annie said, following Drew's gaze.

"Yeah, but it's not frozen over and it's not even raining now," said Drew, hopefully.

"What a beautiful bridge!" said Annie, catching sight of the broad stone arches of the Washington Road Bridge, over which they had just crossed. "And the Gothic tower rising above the trees. It almost looks like England!"

Dr. Dudley narrowed his eyes critically at the scene.

"I believe we shall see all of this from the comfort of the dining room," said Mr. Pipes, leading them through the main entrance.

"But without this infernal wet thing so very near," added Dr. Dudley. "Inside we go and, remember, lunch is on me."

❖ ❖ ❖

"Sorry folks," said a man wearing a white shirt, black trousers, vest, and bow tie and blocking their way to the dining room. He looked like the manager. "We are a *private* rowing club—members only."

Drew looked disappointed.

"Oh, my, yes of course," said Mr. Pipes, touching his forehead. "I should have remembered from my days at Cambridge—that was years ago, mind you. Ah, yes, our little clubhouse was also exclusive of everyone save crew and supporters. Do forgive our intrusion and we'll be off."

"Cambridge did you say?" said the man. "You crewed at Cambridge? Cambridge, England—the University?"

"Well, now yes, but that was more than fifty years ago."

"Hey Bawb!" the man yelled over his shoulder at Bob, who must have been hidden in the kitchen. "I've got an old g—" He halted and looked at Mr. Pipes more closely. "There is a gentleman here used to crew at Cambridge more than fifty years ago. I'm gonna let 'im in. Hey, Sue," he called to a young woman wearing an orange bib apron and holding the menus, "Take good care of these folks."

"Four for lunch?" asked Sue. "You can sit just about wherever you'd like; we have few customers over winter break. What'll it be, close to the fireplace or the windows?"

"Fireplace, if you please," said Dr. Dudley.

"Oh, windows, please," said Drew at the same time.

Dr. Dudley gave Drew a hard stare.

"How about over here," suggested the waitress, leading them through the almost empty club room. "You'll have the fire at your back and a real good view of the lake, and stuff."

They peeled out of their coats and settled into a comfortable table neatly spread with linen and set for lunch. Large oars with black and or-

ange curved blades crisscrossed the stone wall above the mantle lined with gold and silver trophy cups. And a warm fire sizzled and crackled near their table.

"You rowed boats at Cambridge?" asked Annie, when they were seated and Sue left them to study the menu.

"He did," Dr. Dudley answered for Mr. Pipes. "Oxford's the place, and it is the singular impediment to our deepest friendship over the years that he is a Cambridge man. Most shameful!" He opened his menu, scowled at the prices, and grew silent.

Annie and Drew watched Mr. Pipes's eyebrows lift and spread over his open menu; his cheeks rose and his eyes twinkled in a smile.

"Oh, dear me, so many delicious options," he said. "Annie, they have a wonderful-sounding chicken soup with grilled cheese sandwich; that might suit you—do pick whatever you'd like."

Drew swallowed several times and licked his lips as he read the menu descriptions. "… Atlantic Salmon, cold water, fresh caught, marinated in exclusive Princeton Boathouse herb sauce, with savory steamed cockles, garnished with lemon and rosemary, simmered slowly over our special ash-wood fire, roasted potatoes smothered in butter and herbs, your choice of vegetable. Culinary perfection!"

His mouth now crammed with bread stick and butter, Drew asked from behind his menu, "What does c'nary perwection mean?"

"It means it will taste very fine, indeed," explained Mr. Pipes.

"I'm for the Atlantic Salmon," said Mr. Pipes, Dr. Dudley and Drew almost at the same time.

"I just hope they don't simmer it too slowly," added Drew.

"Well, that settles that!" said Mr. Pipes, turning to Annie.

"I'll have the soup and sandwich, please," she said, pulling out her sketchbook. "Isn't this a cozy place, with the fire and all—and we have it almost to ourselves."

While Mr. Pipes and Drew chatted about rowing and crunched on bread sticks, Dr. Dudley, frowning, added up the total for the meal in his address book.

Annie bit her pen cap and repositioned the scrunchy in her blond hair. She twisted her finger round-and-round a wet strand of hair and frowned as she turned page after page of scratched-out poetry in her sketchbook. She needed some kind of inspiration—but it just wasn't there.

🔲 🔲 🔲

The manager with the bow tie helped the waitress set the plates of baked salmon. Drew looked hungrily at the flaky, pink fish swimming in Princeton sauce—steam drifting tantalizingly from it. Annie pushed her sketchbook aside and closed her eyes as she sniffed the steaming broth of her chicken soup; definitely a soup day, she decided.

"S'everything look okay?" the manager asked.

"Culinary perfection!" exclaimed Drew, fork in one hand and knife in the other.

"And sir," he went on to Mr. Pipes, "couple a guys just called to say, what with the mild winter weather right now, they're going to bundle up and get in a few strokes on the lake. Should be here shortly and you'll see 'em r-right out those windows."

After Mr. Pipes offered thanks, Dr. Dudley tucked his linen napkin in his collar and said, "Fall to, then."

For several minutes, one heard only the clinking of forks and knives doing their work, an occasional *ooh*, or *umm*, or *ah* when, accompanied by a head shaken in wonder and eyes lifted to the ceiling, they paused for chewing.

Mr. Pipes broke the silence.

"Now, if my memory of American history serves," he said, dabbing his napkin on his lips, "quite near here, at a place called Trenton, your George Washington crossed the Delaware River Christmas Day and marched through a cold and snowy night, 1776. It was a colder winter than this, as shown in the famous painting commemorating the crossing; the river appears clogged with ice, the men ragged and blue with cold. Blood stained the snow as the demoralized army marched after Washington; two of your Americans actually froze to death in the night. We British didn't expect a holiday attack, especially as Washington's—pardon me for saying so—*ragtag* army was on the run from Lord Cornwallis."

"May he rest in peace," said Dr. Dudley.

"Yeah, isn't he the guy we later romped at Yorktown?" asked Drew, pausing between bites.

"With considerable assistance, I might add," sniffed Dr. Dudley.

"Well, those assisting our side," continued Mr. Pipes, "the German soldiers fighting for hire, lay in their beds recovering from feasting and drinking, confident no army would attack in such cold. Washington desperately needed a victory or he would likely lose most of his army to desertion and despair. At daybreak he commenced a surprise attack with a volley of cannon fire followed by a staggeringly wild charge with only two Americans slightly wounded, and all was over. Washington rounded up nearly a thousand prisoners and wagon loads of much-needed ammunition and supplies—and greatly improved morale among his soldiers."

Mr. Pipes paused, taking another bite of the savory fish.

"Let me get this straight," gasped Dr. Dudley. "The Americans—excuse me children—surprised them in their beds? Dashed cowardly, though not surprising. Pitched battle is the honorable way to kill one's enemies. Colonial wretches, I call them."

"Now wait just a minute," said Drew.

"Hold, my friends," said Mr. Pipes. "Americans had fought Indians for several generations by this time—Indians who knew nothing of our European pitched battles. John Eliot observed, back in 1677, how the first conflicts with the Indians taught the colonists the 'skulking way of war'; and, had they not learned it, Americans would have all died in the wilderness. Battle no longer was a gentleman's pastime; Americans fought for their lives by all tactics.

"Lord Cornwallis was furious and marched determined to 'bag the old fox'—referring to Washington—next morning. Not to be stopped, Washington pretended to dig in for battle through the first part of the night, only to slip around behind the British troops and, once again, surprise them this time by attacking where they least expected it—from behind!"

"Excuse me, miss," said Dr. Dudley, to the waitress. "I believe a very stiff pot of tea might be in order, if you please—a heaping teaspoon of loose-leaf for each cup and one for the pot."

"What happened next?" asked Drew.

Annie sketched away at a drawing of their white-haired friend with the fire and crossed oars in the background.

"It was here that Nassau Hall was taken, lost and retaken by the Americans at the Battle of Princeton a few days later. Brandishing his sword, Washington led a charge into the middle of the British troops and they fled in disarray. Another great victory for the Americans.

"Meanwhile, Princeton's president, the pious patriot, John Witherspoon—descendant of John Knox, and of the Covenanters—earnest and gifted preacher of the gospel, signer of the Declaration of Independence, and member of the first Continental Congress...."

"Wow!" said Drew. "He did a lot."

"He did. Witherspoon—whom Samuel Davies had met in Scotland in 1754 and marked out for a future president of Princeton—preached in the spirit of Samuel Rutherford that 'there is never a single instance in history in which civil liberty was lost and religious liberty preserved entirely.' Many of his students joined the patriot cause, and Princeton became a 'hotbed of radical sentiment' against the British. Mind you, the English had persecuted Presbyterians in Scotland for generations. This was for Witherspoon, perhaps, not entirely a new fight, prompting King George III to call the American War for Independence, the 'Presbyterian parson's war.'"

"You gotta like those Presbyterians," said Drew.

"Pshaw!" snorted Dr. Dudley. "Is that pot of tea about ready, Miss?" And then, under his breath, Annie heard him mutter,

"We'll have our own little tea party right here—humph, at British expense again!"

A few minutes later Annie sipped at her cup of hot tea and nibbled a flat round little cookie. Drew dunked one in his tea and ate it, soft and warm, in one gulp.

"Ahh, that is better," said Dr. Dudley after his first sip.

Drew suddenly jumped up from the table and bolted to the window.

"Hey, look!" he said. "Those guys are carrying a long skinny-looking boat from under us, that must be where they store the boats—and they're plunking the thing into the water."

"Ah, now that brings back memories," said Mr. Pipes, watching the four oarsmen bundled in layers of orange sweaters as they settled gingerly into their rowing stations and fitted long, two-fisted oars into the row locks.

Annie joined Drew and Mr. Pipes at the window.

"Lovely pot of tea," said Dr. Dudley, staying firmly in his seat at the table, his back to the window. "Do make us another."

With measured strokes, the scull[†] pulled from the dock, oars skimming in unison as the oarsmen brought them forward for each new stroke.

"Catching a crab with one of those puppies could send everybody into the drink," observed Drew.

Annie giggled, remembering Drew's first rowing lesson in *Toplady.*

"Knock it off, Annie," said Drew. "I finally got the hang of it."

The scull gained speed and disappeared under an arch of the nearby bridge, and they rejoined Dr. Dudley at the table.

"I don't suppose the boats Washington crossed the Delaware in looked anything like that one," said Drew.

"No, I should think not," said Mr. Pipes.

"So Christians," said Annie, "men like Mr. Witherspoon, actually fought—a-and died in the war?"

---

† A light, narrow racing boat propelled by oars; it is designed for one, two, or sometimes four rowers, each equipped with a pair of oars.

"Indeed, many did," said Mr. Pipes. "Another important Christian patriot minister who served in the war effort was Timothy Dwight, born in Northampton, Massachusetts, in 1752. He inherited the intelligence and diligence of his grandfather, Jonathan Edwards, reading his Bible at the age of four and learning Latin soon after. Later, he graduated from Yale College in Connecticut as a seventeen-year-old, younger than most students when they enter college today. Princeton was actually started in part because, alas, Yale had departed from its early Christian roots and even expelled David Brainard—who would later be Jonathan Edwards's son-in-law and an Indian missionary like Eliot—for what they labeled his 'intemperate, indiscreet zeal.'

"After several years of tutoring at Yale, Dwight was licensed to preach the gospel, and soon after the Battle of Princeton, he joined the Patriot Army as a chaplain. Always first and foremost a lover of Christ's Church and Kingdom. Yet, with a strong sense of his spiritual duties, Dwight eventually left the army when his father died in 1778. He returned home to work and support his mother and twelve younger siblings."

"Left the army, did you say?" said Dr. Dudley, leaning forward with interest. "Perhaps there's hope for this one."

"Thirteen kids!" said Annie. "What would his mother do back in those days when her husband died?"

"Precisely," said Mr. Pipes. "That is why Timothy gave up his inheritance as the eldest son and cared for his family sacrificially for as long as they needed him. For years he ministered in a church at Greenfield, Connecticut, where he started a Christian school in which hundreds of boys and girls received a biblical education. He showed considerable poetic abilities while serving at Greenfield and, no doubt, taught his students how to write in verse and meter."

"Like you've been doing with us," said Annie. Then she added forlornly, "Only I'm not getting it very well."

"You're doing lots better than me," said Drew.

"'Than I' you mean, my boy," said Mr. Pipes. "Patience, my dear Annie. Great poetry is not made overnight, nor without considerable effort."

Frowning, Annie studied the first line of the poem she had tried starting.

Mr. Pipes continued: "Yale College eventually called Pastor Dwight to be president. His leadership and zealous preaching prompted a revival of true faith among students and faculty, and a return to the orthodox Calvinism so much a feature of Jonathan Edwards's ministry and of the founding Puritans of the American colonies.

"But perhaps his greatest contribution to the church," continued Mr. Pipes, after another sip of tea, "was his appointment in 1797 to edit and complete Isaac Watts' Psalm versifications in a new American addition."

"Why did they need an American version?" asked Drew.

"Watts made a few too many references to England and the king in his hymns," said Mr. Pipes. "Colonists resented this."

"I'll bet we did," said Drew.

"Versification," said Annie, "that's when you use a particular Psalm to write the hymn, isn't it?"

"Yes. You will remember that Isaac Watts took many more liberties with the Psalms by actually interpreting them in his poetry."

"Yeah," said Drew. "He added Jesus' name to Psalms that didn't use His name but prophesied His coming to save us. I remember that."

"Mr. Dwight not only edited Watts's Psalms but added hymns, based on Psalms, of his own to the collection. His finest hymn, 'I Love Thy Kingdom, Lord,' was later set to John Stainer's simple but timeless musical setting, *Veni*."

"*Sir* John Stainer," said Dr. Dudley, sitting up abruptly. "He is an Englishman, a knight of the realm—and an Oxford man. I am sure it is a perfect musical setting."

"It does suit Dwight's poetry well and serves as an enhancement to Christian worship," said Mr. Pipes.

"How's it go?" said Drew.

Mr. Pipes softly hummed the music. Annie thought it sounded peaceful but at the same time there was something unshakable about it.

"What does the poetry sound like?" she asked.

"It is a very intimate prayer, yet one all earnest Christians can pray," said Mr. Pipes, steepling his fingers and looking at the ceiling. "Let me see if I can recollect it."

As he began reciting the hymn, Drew thought Mr. Pipes sounded like he was really praying the words:

> I love Thy Kingdom, Lord,
> The house of Thine abode,
> The church our blest Redeemer saved
> With His own precious blood.
>
> I love Thy church, O God:
> Her walls before Thee stand,
> Dear as the apple of Thine eye,
> And graven on Thy hand.

He paused. "Now that much of the hymn is taken from Psalm 26:8, but Mr. Dwight is so full of the Bible that these verses also borrow generously from other biblical allusions. Notice how full his hymn is of doctrinal truth and clear-sighted devotion. The rest goes like this:

> For her my tears shall fall,
> For her my prayers ascend;
> To her my cares and toils be giv'n,
> Till toils and cares shall end.

Annie thought of John Eliot's long life of toil for the salvation of the Indians. Mr. Dwight must have been like that, too, she decided.

> Beyond my highest joy
> I prize her heavenly ways,

Her sweet communion, solemn vows,
Her hymns of love and praise.

"Words penned by a man," said Mr. Pipes, "who understood
how much worship ought to be a foretaste of heavenly delights.
Now, notice his confidence in the final lines of this prayer:"

Jesus, Thou Friend Divine,
Our Savior and our King,
Thy hand from ev'ry snare and foe
Shall great deliv'rance bring.

Sure as thy truth shall last,
To Zion shall be giv'n
The brightest glories earth can yield,
And brighter bliss of heav'n.

The fire crackled comfortingly nearby as Annie and Drew sat
in silence, wondering at Mr. Dwight's love for Christ and His
body, the church.

"Though everything about your world says the contrary, my
dears," said Mr. Pipes, at last. "Your devoted membership to the
church and your heartfelt participation in her worship is the
source of the 'brightest glories'—the most satisfying pleasure in
this world and in your life to come in heaven. You see, you will
be doing perfectly in heaven what we aspire to do in our worship
here on earth. And, oh, alas, my dears, our worship is all too
earthbound. But when we do raise our voices, singing with the
church 'hymns of love and praise' worthy of God, we are closest
to the heavenly life we will enjoy for all eternity, filled with never-
ending pleasure at the Lord's right hand—the 'brightest bliss of
heaven.' I believe Mr. Dwight understood all this, and he certainly does now and has since his death from cancer in 1817."

A few moments later, after the last of the tea disappeared, Drew caught sight of the rowing scull shooting out from under the bridge. He ran to the window followed by all but Dr. Dudley.

"Boy, I sure would like to try that!" he said. "Is it lots harder than rowing *Toplady*, Mr. Pipes?"

"Well, with this kind of rowing you operate only one oar," said Mr. Pipes. "However, one must row in perfect harmony with everyone else. That can be the rather tricky bit. Oh, yes, and this sort of rowing is considerably faster than the speed—or lack thereof—of which my dear *Toplady* is capable."

"Faster, huh?" said Drew, looking longingly down at the boat.

They watched the manager come out onto the dock and speak with the crew as they pulled their scull alongside. He turned and gestured toward the window several times, then he left them and soon appeared upstairs.

"Now, sir, you have rowed a boat," he began, smiling at them. "How 'bout the rest of you?"

"The children have developed some degree of ability in a rowing boat," said Mr. Pipes, hesitantly. "But neither have ever properly crewed. And, mind you, it has been many years since I—"

"Hey, that's good enough for me. Listen, I've got a proposal for you," continued the manager, waving his hand as if to brush aside Mr. Pipes's reluctance. "The boys down there are itching for a little off-season race; I've got a four-man scull for you; I'll be your coxswain[†] and we'll see how a Cambridge man does against Princeton. Lunch is on the house, win or lose. Wha'd'ya say?"

Mr. Pipes looked wide-eyed; but, before he could refuse, Drew chimed in, "You've got yourself a deal! We'd love to!"

Dr. Dudley bit his lip. He hated boats and water, but what did the fellow say about lunch on the house? Here was a way he could get out of paying for lunch. He scowled and twisted his finger around his moustache and pulled.

[†] The steersman of a racing shell; the word *coxswain* comes from a small vessel called a "cock boat" and a country boy or servant called a "swain."

"Ahem, I don't suppose," said Dr. Dudley, hopefully, "that, ah, your offer stands if just my three companions were to row?"

"Not a chance," said the manager with a laugh. "That'd be like rowing with one oar in the water." He spun his finger around in circles.

Mr. Pipes, who felt himself warming to the idea of a good row, pulled Dr. Dudley aside and whispered in his ear, "I say, dear fellow, I do believe, though the children are Americans, our honor as Englishmen—perhaps yours as an Oxford man, even—is at stake. I think we cannot refuse. And you might just find that you enjoy rowing."

"Oh, I assure you," said Dr. Dudley, looking narrowly at his friend, "I will *do* it, but it is simply out of the question that I will *enjoy* doing it. Carry on, let us get this over with—and hope we don't all drown; don't say I did not warn you if we do."

The manager, who introduced himself as Jack, decided Mr. Pipes should sit in the forward seat, Annie and Drew amidships and Dr. Dudley in the stern facing Jack, the coxswain in charge of steering and the only one in the boat looking where they were going.

"It is such a dashed backward activity, rowing," sniffed Dr. Dudley as he stepped gingerly into the scull.

"Don't step on your seat!" yelled Jack, at Dr. Dudley. "They slide; you'd a been in the drink in a heartbeat."

"Couldn't they properly attach the thing so that it jolly well doesn't slide?" questioned Dr. Dudley, lowering himself awkwardly into the narrow seat.

Annie and Drew felt their hearts quicken in anticipation as they sat down—Drew with an orange and black bladed starboard oar, Annie with a port.

Mr. Pipes straightened his tie and turned up the collar of his wool greatcoat against the cold in preparation to step aboard.

The four Princeton crewmen stood grinning at the spectacle and at Dr. Dudley's protests.

"All right," said Jack, stepping nimbly into the coxswain's seat and fitting a megaphone into a holder so that he could call "*Stroke!*" while using his hands for steering at the same time. "Princeton'll give you a one-hundred-yard handicap before they begin—since you're a little out of practice. Every time I say 'stroke,' you dip the blade of your oar in the water then pull with your arms and push with your feet. Nothing to it!"

"May I make so bold as to request several yards of practice stroking?" inquired Mr. Pipes. Then to Annie and Drew he whispered, "Remember all I taught you on *Toplady*, and let each one do his best; I expect no less."

"*Stroke! Stroke! Stroke!*" Jack's voice boomed as they at first splashed and wobbled toward the bridge.

"I say—puff, puff," came Dr. Dudley's voice. "Who is the blighter rocking this infernal boat?"

"'fraid it's you," said Jack, between strokes. "Every time you look over your shoulder—*Stroke!*—you upset the balance—*Stroke!*—and you miss your stroke—*Stroke!*—Let *me* do the steering; you just *row*—*Stroke!*"

Eventually they wobbled less and actually began slicing more steadily through the water. Drew thought he heard Dr. Dudley making little grunts of pleasure like, "hmm, aha," and so forth, as he seemed to gain confidence. Gripping his oar with both hands, Drew felt the leveraged power as he pulled on the long, well-balanced sweep, and the scull surged through the water. He stole a sideways glance at the trees rushing by on shore.

"We're flying!" he called.

"Aha! Indeed," called Dr. Dudley over his shoulder.

But then Drew caught sight of a streak of orange coming from nowhere and shooting like a rocket toward their starboard quarter.

"Yes, yes," said Mr. Pipes. "However, Princeton, it would appear, is flying a bit faster."

Annie whispered to Drew on the next stroke, "Did you ever think we'd get Dr. Dudley in a boat?"

"No way," replied Drew. "And I'll bet he is enjoying it."

"Pull, mates, pull!" called Dr. Dudley, through gritted teeth. "They'll beat us over my lifeless corpse. *Pull*, I say; Britannia rules the sea!"

I Love Thy Kingdom, Lord

I love the house where you live, O LORD, the place where your glory dwells. Ps. 26:8

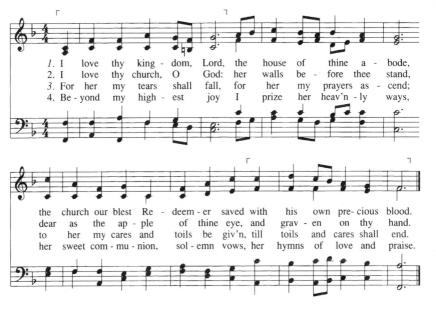

1. I love thy king - dom, Lord, the house of thine a - bode,
2. I love thy church, O God: her walls be - fore thee stand,
3. For her my tears shall fall, for her my prayers as - cend;
4. Be - yond my high - est joy I prize her heav'n - ly ways,

the church our blest Re - deem - er saved with his own pre - cious blood.
dear as the ap - ple of thine eye, and grav - en on thy hand.
to her my cares and toils be giv'n, till toils and cares shall end.
her sweet com - mu - nion, sol - emn vows, her hymns of love and praise.

5. Jesus, thou Friend divine,
   our Savior and our King,
   thy hand from ev'ry snare and foe
   shall great deliv'rance bring.

6. Sure as thy truth shall last,
   to Zion shall be giv'n
   the brightest glories earth can yield,
   and brighter bliss of heav'n.

Timothy Dwight, 1800

ST. THOMAS S.M.
Aaron Williams, 1763

This is the first stanza of the national anthem of the
United States, exactly as Francis Scott Key penned it on
September 14, 1814. The night before, he had been de-
tained on board a prisoner exchange ship, while seeking
the release of a friend. Key anxiously watched as the British bombarded Fort McHenry, near Baltimore, Mary-
land. In the morning, Key was elated to see that his
country's "flag was still there," which inspired him to
write "The Star-Spangled Banner." This poem officially
became America's national anthem in 1931.

Chapter Five

Francis Scott Key
1779-1843

Let Thy love, my soul's chief treasure,
Love's pure flame within me raise;
And, since words can never measure,
Let my life show forth Thy praise.

Dr. Dudley's pleasure at not paying for lunch seemed overshadowed by the fact that Mr. Pipes and Annie and Drew knew he had actually enjoyed an activity for which he previously held nothing but scorn. This troubled him that night on the train to Boston. He frequently furrowed his brow and gazed resolutely out of the window through rapidly blinking eyes, his moustache undergoing regular twists and yanks. No doubt, his English honor also smarted from the trouncing they received from the Princeton crew. Annie and Drew overheard him reasoning to himself, "'Twas my first go, and they've been at it for years; put them alongside an experienced Oxford crew, now, that would be a jolly sight, indeed." He sniffed a good deal, and the others left him to recover a dignity badly bruised, but not beyond recovery.

"Two days down," said Drew, chin on his hand, and gazing out the window of the train at white Christmas lights outlining the gables of passing houses, "and only two left. Do you still think it'll snow, Mr. Pipes."

"I do," said the old man with a determined nod of his white head.

"But," said Annie, with a sigh, "before we go home?"

"Well, now, that I cannot say. However, it would seem something of a waste to spend the remaining two days discussing the inexorable passage of time instead of simply enjoying what time we do have. Don't you agree?"

They agreed.

After several minutes of companionable silence in the dim light of the train (silence, except for Drew crunching loudly on a bag of corn nuts) as it sped toward Boston, Annie said:

"What did Mr. Dwight mean with the phrase, 'The church our blest Redeemer saved with His own precious blood?' That seems to leave a lot of people out; what about the rest of the world; wasn't Jesus' blood for them, too?"

For a moment, Mr. Pipes stared at her over his glasses and through his bushy brows. After running his fingers through his snowy hair, he replied, "My dear, God from all eternity set His church apart from the world to be the 'apple of His eye.' That is to say, He chose us by His matchless grace then redeemed us as His special favorites. I am sure that you and Drew understand what it is to be someone's special favorite, do you not, my dear?" he concluded, with a smile.

Annie looked up at Mr. Pipes in the dimness; a passing signal light sparkled in his kind eyes. She snuggled against the tweed of his shoulder.

Drew stopped chewing for a moment.

Mr. Pipes continued: "Samuel Davies expressed the same truth when he wrote, 'Pardon bestowed through Jesus' blood!' The unbelieving world does not desire nor is marked out for pardon through Jesus' blood. But His church is pardoned, and you and I are the objects of this distinguishing love, my dears. This is grace unbought and undeserved, 'grace so rich and free,' for a vast multitude who have been called out of the world."

"I-it makes sense," said Drew, soberly. "If it's grace, then it can't be anything we do or deserve, right?"

"True, my boy," said Mr. Pipes. "We are, first to last sinners sought, bought, and brought to salvation by God's doing. And since God found us and roused us from our sins and placed His blood-sealed pardon on us, we ought to overflow with the deepest and most devout praise. Your early American hymn writers followed this biblical understanding championed by John Calvin in the Reformation and expressed by the Psalmist in Psalm 119:54, 'Your decrees are the theme of my song.'"

"That'd be Geneva," said Drew. "You told us all about Calvin and the Psalter last summer."

Annie thought longingly of their friends on the farm near Geneva and of a certain kitten growing into "cathood."

"Calvinism," said Mr. Pipes, "is the theological fabric out of which Davies, Dwight, and others wove their hymns."

"Mr. Eliot, too?" asked Annie.

"Mr. Eliot, most certainly," replied Mr. Pipes. "Now, let us rest as best we can before Boston."

◈ ◈ ◈

Next morning, as they sat looking out the frosty window of a café on Snowhill Street, waiting for their bacon and eggs, Drew exclaimed, "I could eat a horse!"

"Drink your tea, Drew," said Dr. Dudley. "I doubt even colonial eating establishments serve horse meat."

"Look, the sun is trying to break through the clouds," said Annie, changing the subject.

"And just across that cemetery," said Mr. Pipes, pointing north out the window, "is Boston Harbor."

"Where we had the tea party!" said Drew, looking sideways at Dr. Dudley.

"Party? Humph!" snorted Dr. Dudley, his teacup clattering onto its saucer. "Your kind defied the king, vandalized his Majesty's ships and *stole*—mind you, *stole*—his tea, perfectly *good* tea! No wonder we felt compelled to come over and give you what for."

Drew smiled.

"Now in fairness, my friend," said Mr. Pipes. "The Boston Tea Party was a political statement in an effort to awaken the British crown to colonial concerns over taxes and their denied rights to representation as British subjects. One Loyalist even admitted that the Boston Tea Party was a crime 'conducted as correctly as a crime could be.' The patriots, dressed as Mohawk Indians and to shouts of, 'Boston Harbor, a teapot tonight!' boarded three ships and summarily dumped 342 large containers of premium tea into the harbor, just there." He nodded toward the waterfront down the street.

"Wasteful impudence!" said Dr. Dudley.

"They stole nothing," continued Mr. Pipes, "even replaced a damaged padlock and swept the decks before leaving the scene. Then they marched away singing something to the effect:

> Rally, Mohawks! Bring out your axes,
> And tell King George, we'll pay no more taxes."

"Would that be good poetry?" asked Annie.

"Ah, well," said Mr. Pipes. "Let us say it served its purpose."

"What happened next?" asked Drew, sniffing the air as the fresh scent of frying bacon sizzled from the kitchen.

"Some time later at a convention in Virginia called to discuss how best to turn farmers into fighting militias, an eloquent lawyer named Patrick Henry rose to his feet and gave an impassioned speech ending—"

Annie and Drew cut him off and recited together, "'—Give me liberty, or give me death!'"

"That's sort of like poetry, isn't it?" said Annie.

"Very like," said Mr. Pipes. "Mr. Henry learned some of his command of words from Samuel Davies's preaching. And Patrick Henry—with a daughter named 'Annie,' Annie—perhaps the most powerful orator of American liberty, called Davies the greatest orator of all."

▧ ▧ ▧

After breakfast, and while waiting for a cab to carry them across the Charlestown Bridge, Mr. Pipes pointed down the street at the colonial brick Old North Church, its clean white steeple rising into the broken winter clouds above.

"'Listen, my children, and you shall hear,'" quoted Mr. Pipes, and the children joined in, "'Of the midnight ride of Paul Revere.'"

They laughed together—all but Dr. Dudley, that is.

Mr. Pipes continued, "'One if by land, and two, if by sea.' You remember the story immortalized by Henry Wadsworth Longfellow, one of America's greatest poets. With 'muffled oar' Revere was 'rowed to the Charlestown shore,' just over there." He pointed toward the Charlestown Navy Yard. "There he awaited the lantern signal from the church belfry."

"It was two lanterns—so 'by sea,' right?" said Drew.

"Yes," said Mr. Pipes. "If the British had not come down the Charles River as they did—by sea, they would have passed through Roxbury, John Eliot's village, south of Boston."

"And it would have been only one lantern," said Annie.

"Yes," said Mr. Pipes. "And from Charlestown, with the 'hurry of hoofs,' Revere spurred his horse into action. That night he rallied hundreds of minutemen who next day defeated the British at Concord Bridge, where 'the shot heard round the world' was fired."

"Now, Longfellow wrote real poetry," said Annie. "But not exactly hymn poetry."

"No, indeed, my dear," said Mr. Pipes. "And, I say, it is most important to discern the difference."

Their taxi arrived and the cabdriver, his cellular phone crammed to his ear, greeted them with a curt, "Where does you's wants to go, huh?"

"We are off to the USS *Constitution*, if you please, sir," said Mr. Pipes.

"Yeah, yeah, sure, I knows d'place."

Mr. Pipes had barely closed the door before the cab squealed away from the curb. Moments later the cab screeched to a halt and deposited them, somewhat ruffled, at the navy yard pier. Three enormous white masts crossed with black yardarms and held taut with a spider-web labyrinth of standing rigging, rose from the menacing black hulk of a great ship. Old Glory snapped in the December breeze near the boomkin.

"Now, I really do not believe," said Dr. Dudley, dusting the sleeves of his wool coat and scowling after the rapidly disappearing cab, "that ride was any better than my driving."

Not commenting, Mr. Pipes led them toward the ship.

"Whoa! They've got her ready for action!" said Drew, admiring the dizzyingly complex rigging, the open gun ports and rows of all-business looking cannons threatening from her topsides.

"Indeed," said Mr. Pipes. "With her enormous bowsprit[†] facing the sea, as it is, she looks eager to slip her moorings and, once again, stalk the main, defending your liberties."

"She's way bigger and tougher looking than the *Mayflower*," said Drew. "I like her, big time."

Dr. Dudley slowed as he took in the American flag, the guns, and the American sailors standing guard at the gangway.

"Now, wait just one moment," he said, stopping short. The others turned. "Is this, may I inquire, an *actual* American war ship, not a replica?"

"Indeed, it is," said Mr. Pipes, smiling at the well-maintained vessel. "She is the oldest naval vessel afloat in the entire world, and though kept now as a symbol of American freedom, in her fighting days the USS *Constitution* never saw defeat in a single battle."

"Impressive!" said Drew, as they came alongside, the stout planking of the ship rising high overhead.

"And you, dear man," said Dr. Dudley, "an Englishman, plan to board her and *ooh* and *ah* over her guns and decks, likely as not, forever stained with the blood of your own countrymen. Shocking disloyalty! Will you confirm or deny that those very cannons have ever been the cause of the death of one Englishman over the years? I await an immediate answer."

"Well, my dear Dr. Dudley," replied Mr. Pipes. "*Old Ironsides*, as she is affectionately called, in former days might have actually been called the very scourge of the British Navy. But, my dear fellow, you—"

---

† A spar projecting from the upper end of the bow, or front, of a sailing vessel.

"I'll hear no more," said Dr. Dudley, raising his hand in protest. "The word *treason* comes to mind when I think of you boarding said vessel and actually entertaining yourself with the enemy. But I can see you are determined. I, for one, will not stoop!" And he turned on his heel and began walking toward a collection of nearby skyscrapers.

"Dr. Dudley, where are you going?" called Annie.

"No offense intended, my dear, but I cannot, like some, violate my loyalties [sniff, sniff]. I will, therefore, simply angle my way to a nearby tea room, or some such thing, whilst you all revel in American glories—*past* glories, I might be tempted to add."

And he was gone.

"Perhaps, he grows a trifle weary of American history," said Mr. Pipes. "Time on his own, poor chap, will do wonders, I assure you. We'll not recognize the man when he returns. Now, then, prepare for boarding!"

Annie wrapped her wool scarf around her neck against the cold as they stepped on to the tidy decks.

"This thing looks battle ready!" said Drew, fingering the tarred ratlines and looking aloft enviously. "And these guys are real sailors—least they sure do look like the real thing."

"Now, you mean this isn't built just to look like a real fighting ship," said Annie. "It actually was used to fight … a-and men might have d-died on her decks?"

"Indeed," said Mr. Pipes, patting Annie's shoulder.

"Was she used in the Revolution?" asked Drew.

"No, my boy," said Mr. Pipes. "Your revolution ended with the defeat of my ancestors, the treaty signed ending the war in 1783. This fine vessel was launched in 1797 and has been in almost continuous use ever since."

"I say we put it to use right now," said Drew. "No chance, do you think, Mr. Pipes, of them giving us a quick spin around the harbor?"

"None, entirely," said Mr. Pipes.

"I was afraid of that," said Drew, running his hand along the shiny black cap rail.

"Did you say 1797?" continued Drew. "That makes this ship more than 200 years old!"

"It does," replied Mr. Pipes.

"But, if the Revolution was over," said Annie, "when did America use this ship against the British?"

Drew, with the side of his face plastered tight against the mainmast, reached his arms around the base of the giant spar. Though he clutched and strained, he couldn't clasp or even touch his gloved hands.

"Big as trees," he said, rubbing his cold cheek.

"Well, I'm afraid we British," continued Mr. Pipes, "didn't take the new little American States very seriously. By 1812, our side had developed the nasty habit of boarding your ships, seizing cargo and often conscripting your sailors."

"Oh, that seems kind of mean," said Annie.

"I wholeheartedly agree, my dear," said Mr. Pipes. "And I assure you, though British, I never would have participated in such doings."

A smartly dressed sailor, wearing a black pea coat, led them below to the gun deck. Light and some of the cold wind made its way through the gun ports, but it was warmer there.

"Check out these cannons!" said Drew, eyeing down a shiny black barrel. "There's tons of 'em. Couldn't they do some damage?"

"Oh, and did!" said Mr. Pipes.

Their sailor guide told them how over 6,000 American seaman had been effectively stolen and forced into service in the British Navy and how over 1,000 ships had been seized. He also told how President James Madison finally declared war on the British in 1812 and how *Old Ironsides* got its nickname against the HMS *Guerrière*.

"Tubs of water," continued the sailor, "were filled for putting out fires and for thirsty sailors to drink from during the engagement. Gunners removed the tampions[†] from their cannons and

---

† A plug placed in the muzzle of a piece of a ordinance to keep it free of moisture and dirt, when it is not in use.

made ready, while barefoot boys carried gunpowder from the powder magazine further below."

"Why barefoot," asked Annie.

"Blow the whole ship up if a nail from someone's boot made friction against the floor of the powder magazine—those sorts of things did happen," said the sailor, knowingly. "Then they sprinkled sand all over the gun decks."

"What for?" asked Drew.

The sailor looked at Annie before answering.

"U.S. sailors were wounded on these decks that day," he said, "and a number killed. The blood of the dead and dying make a deck pretty slippery; sand helped the men keep their footing and continue fighting."

Annie looked wide-eyed down the shafts of gray light filtering in the gun ports and casting eerie shadows across the silent decks. She swallowed as the sailor continued.

"On deck, sailors readied sails and rigging for action, while drummers beat the signal 'to quarters.' One gunner, Moses Smith, recalled in his journal, 'quick as thought, studding sails snapped to, fore and aft. The noble frigate fairly bounded over the billows.' Captain Isaac Hull moved among his men tensely waiting for action. 'Men, now do your duty,' he said. 'Each man must do all in his power for his country.' Then he boomed in command, 'Sailing master! Lay her alongside!'

"*Constitution* heeled eagerly toward the *Guerrière*; and, as the distance closed, Captain Hull shouted, 'Now, boys, hull her!' They held steady until the British ship crested a wave and heeled away on the downward roll, her undersides exposed. Then, to the cadence of the gun captains, '*Stop vent! Sponge! Load! Run out your guns! FIRE!*' with a deafening roar, *Constitution* sent a terrifying volley of cannon fire into the hull of the Britisher—below the waterline where it would do the most damage."

Drew could hardly contain himself and ran from gun to gun, eyeing through the gun ports and seeing the great battle as if he were in it.

The thrill of the story for Annie was dulled as she thought about the men on both sides who died that day. Pulling out her sketchbook with a sigh, she sat down on a gun carriage. Maybe a battle like this might inspire some people to write poetry, but she felt too sad about it all.

"Both crews worked furiously, each cannon firing every minute and a half. Meanwhile, the crew of the *Guerrière* watched in wonder as cannon balls shot at point-blank range harmlessly bounced off *Constitution's* hull. One gunner reportedly cried, 'Look, her sides are made of iron!'"

"Aha! That's where her nickname, *Old Ironsides*, came from," said Drew. "But why didn't cannon balls hurt her?"

"Special kind of oak—St. Simon's Island oak," said the sailor, rapping his knuckles soundlessly on the curved insides of the hull, then shaking his hand in mock pain. "Tougher than anything. And her planking is two feet thick of it. Took 1,500 oak trees to build her, cut from about sixty acres of forest in Georgia."

"She's massive," said Drew. "What happened next?"

"After a constant hail of 953 rounds from *Constitution's* guns, what remained of *Guerrière's* fore and mainmasts littered the waves and her bloody decks; the sea gushed in her splintered and listing hull. The wounded British captain reluctantly surrendered, and the crew of the *Constitution* gave three hearty cheers in celebration of victory and in remembrance of their dead comrades. Captain Hull turned to his sailing master and said, ''Tis a good day's work.'

"In 1830," continued their guide, "after many more victories, careless politicians wanted to scuttle the aging ship; that's when the poet, Oliver Wendell Holmes, wrote a scathing poetic protest that inflamed Americans with patriotic zeal to keep this proud vessel as a memorial. He wrote:

> Her deck, once stained with heroes' blood,
> Where knelt the vanquished foe,
> When winds were hurrying o'er the flood
> And waves were white below,

No more shall feel the victor's tread,
Or know the conquered knee....

"'Tis best Dr. Dudley is not here," whispered Mr. Pipes to Annie. "I fear, t'would strain his disposition."

They thanked the young seaman for his story, and he left them to explore.

▩ ▩ ▩

"So, what happened next in the War of 1812?" asked Drew. "And did we whoop the Brit—Oh, sorry, Mr. Pipes?"

"We British did capture Washington, your national capital," said Mr. Pipes. "But you Americans, I fear, soundly frustrated our all-out efforts to split the nation in two by capturing the strategic Fort McHenry and Baltimore, just north on the Chesapeake Bay."

"Tell us about that fight," begged Drew.

Mr. Pipes looked at Annie. "My dear, this battle story leads us to poetry—poetry put to its highest purpose."

"Oh, then I'd like to hear about it, too," she said.

Mr. Pipes sat next to Annie on the gun carriage and began:

"September 13, 1814, our British fleet lay in battle position arrayed against Fort McHenry, when a sloop[†] flying a flag of truce came alongside the warship of the commander of the British Army and Navy. The commander cordially greeted Francis Scott Key, a young Washington lawyer who had come to negotiate the release of his friend, an elderly American doctor, held prisoner on the British ship. They agreed to release the doctor but refused to let the party sail back to shore because the fleet bristled with preparations for a nighttime bombardment of the American fort."

"So Francis Scott Key and the doctor had to stay on a British ship during the battle?" asked Annie. "That must have been a little awkward."

---

† A small sailing vessel that is a single-masted, fore-and-aft-rigged boat.

"Yeah, but maybe they sabotaged the British guns, or some-thing," said Drew.

"No British general worth his salt would have allowed that, my boy," said Mr. Pipes. "But, they did have front-row seats of the battle as twilight descended into night and British shells hammered the little fort in the darkness. At times, in 'the rockets' red glare' as bombs burst in mid air, Key and his companion took courage as they caught glimpses of the American flag, tattered but still flying over the fort. First light next morning, Mr. Key saw that the flag was, in fact, still there, flying 'o're the land of the free and the home of the brave.' The British attack had failed. He felt a wave of relief, and a surge of patriotic inspiration overcame him. He grabbed an envelope and scribbled out a poem, later called 'The Star-Spangled Banner,' your national anthem. Once on shore, he added more verses wherein he praised 'the Pow'r that hath made and preserved us a nation.' He concludes his poem with the suggestion that America's motto ought to be—'In God is our trust.' Which of course," Mr. Pipes continued, pulling out a twenty dollar bill, "said motto appears, perhaps a bit ironically, just here and on all your money."

Drew read, "'In God We Trust.'" And then he added, "Hmm, that's odd; they've got it printed over The White House."

"I'm afraid most of America doesn't really trust in God," said Annie. She bit her lower lip and continued. "Mr. Pipes, Drew and I want our Mom and Dad to really trust in God—to know they're sinners, a-and to know all about God's grace. But I never know quite how to talk to them about it all. We're really hoping you can help us during your visit."

"Yeah," said Drew. "When I try to explain it, Mom says things like, 'That's nice for you, just don't get too carried away with your religious ideas, as if yours were the only ones.' She says something like that."

"God has graciously given the light of the Gospel to you, my dears," said Mr. Pipes, kindly, "But He has not yet given spiri-tual light to your parents; we must continue to pray and trust that He will."

"But what if He doesn't; what else can we do?" asked Annie, in earnest.

"Trusting in God," replied Mr. Pipes, "means resting in His sovereign will for your parents' salvation. Do keep searching God's Word and speaking of your faith to them, and continue praying—remember, they cannot be saved unless God changes their hearts, like He did yours. But most importantly, Annie, Drew, let your lives show forth His praise; live out your trust in God in thought, word, and deed."

Drew crossed his arms, and leaning on a cannon, he shifted his weight from foot to foot. He suddenly thought of all kinds of ways he could be living out his praise to God—but wasn't!

"Three years after Fort McHenry," continued Mr. Pipes a moment later, "Francis Scott Key put his poetic abilities to a far higher use and penned one of America's finest hymns. In it he sings of sin and guilt, of grace and pardon, of love and obedience, all leading to the highest and deepest praise. Mr. Key created a Psalm-like theological argument for why our lives ought to be overflowing with enraptured praise."

"So *he* definitely trusted in God," said Drew.

"Indeed."

"I'd like to hear his hymn," said Annie.

"Here it is," said Mr. Pipes, "but notice carefully how his praise flows from the many objective reasons for that praise." He then added sadly, "This is miles from the empty pop praise that passes for worship today." His voice then rose throughout the gun deck of the old fighting ship, whose guns echoed long ago during Francis Scott Key's own lifetime:

> Lord, with glowing heart I'd praise thee,
> For the bliss thy love bestows,
> For the pard'ning grace that saves me,
> And the peace that from it flows:
> Help, O God, my weak endeavor;
> This dull soul to rapture raise:

Thou must light the flame, or never
Can my love be warmed to praise.

Praise, my soul, the God that sought thee,
Wretched wand'rer far astray;
Found thee lost, and kindly brought thee
From the paths of death away:

Mr. Pipes paused for a moment, and Annie remembered John Newton's hymn about wretches saved by amazing grace.

Praise, with love's devoutest feeling,
Him who saw thy guilt-born fear,
And, the light of hope revealing,
Bade the blood-stain'd cross appear.

Praise thy Savior God that drew thee
To that cross, new life to give,
Held a blood-sealed pardon to thee,
Bade thee look at him and live:
Praise the grace whose threats alarmed thee,
Roused thee from thy fatal ease,
Praise the grace whose promise warm'd thee,
Praise the grace that whispered peace.

Drew bit the inside of his cheek as he listened intently. He decided that Mr. Key must have been a Calvinist because he describes salvation as God doing everything—"Drawing me, pardoning me, showing me my sins and the punishment I deserve. Giving me peace with God...."

"And now this last verse," said Mr. Pipes. "In it Mr. Key prays—and we with him—for the deepest worship, full of the most appropriate feeling for one redeemed and pardoned from so great a guilt as that from which we have been delivered." He continued,

Lord, this bosom's ardent feeling
Vainly would my lips express:

Low before thy footstool kneeling,
Deign thy suppliant's pray'r to bless:
Let thy love, my soul's chief treasure,
Love's pure flame within me raise;
And, since words can never measure,
Let my life show forth thy praise.

"That was the phrase you said just a minute ago about our witness to Mom and Dad," said Annie. "Let our lives show forth His praise; you were quoting this hymn."

"I was," said Mr. Pipes simply.

"I think you do that a lot," said Annie, smiling at their friend.

"No doubt," chuckled Mr. Pipes. "But I only do so because good hymns bring together, with beauty and brevity, what God has said is true in His Word."

◈ ◈ ◈

Back on the pier, a red pickup truck lurched toward them down the street—wandering frequently to the left side of the centerline.

"Wh-what on earth!" said Mr. Pipes, as the truck jerked to a halt.

The driver scooted across from the steering wheel and got out on the passenger side.

"It's Dr. Dudley!" said Annie in amazement.

"What ho! Pipes!" said Dr. Dudley, coming toward them with an enormous grin. "Here, Americans might just have one thing to offer the world—personal lorries—pickup trucks, they call them. I realize, a most American phenomenon, but, I have quite decided that no place is all bad—and, well [sniff], I rather like it," he concluded looking proudly at the truck.

"Wow! Dr. Dudley," said Drew.

"My dear fellow," said Mr. Pipes, his white eyebrows furrowed as he scowled at the vehicle. "You didn't purchase this monstrosity? Tell me you didn't. A-and what is all that stuff in the back of the thing?"

"Hired," said Dr. Dudley, disappointedly. "Now, look here, Mr. Pipes," he continued, taking his elderly friend by the arm and leading him closer to the pickup. "I happened upon a copy of the *Boston Globe*, they rather exaggeratingly call it; there is a winter storm warning afoot, and I found this most interesting article on how one prepares for such things. One is advised to drive only stout vehicles."

"Thus the American pickup, I presume," said Mr. Pipes.

"Precisely," Dr. Dudley went on, patting the hood affectionately with his gloved hand. "It is most exciting. We are advised to stock up on groceries, which I have taken the liberty—this being America, and all that rot—of doing."

He pulled back a canvas that covered the bed of the pickup, revealing several cases of canned food, boxes of crackers, eggs, smoked hams, bottles of ginger ale, distilled water, a box of candles, a case of matches and several tins of loose-leaf tea.

"I've done precisely what the article suggested," he said almost gleefully. "So, we'll be right as rain in any storm."

"What's all the other stuff?" asked Annie.

"Ah, sleeping bags," said Dr. Dudley, knowingly. Then with a slap of the back of his hand against the newspaper, he explained, "Do you realize people freeze to death in their automobiles in winter storms, but not those who heed advice and carry sleeping bags, no indeed, and I have got them—one for each of us."

Mr. Pipes took the newspaper from Dr. Dudley and began reading the article.

"What's the rope for?" asked Drew. "Say, did you get any fishing gear?"

"How is one to fish," replied Dr. Dudley, "when ice and snow covers all?"

Drew looked disappointed. "Well," he concluded, "you must have spent a fortune on all this stuff."

"Our very lives could be at stake," replied Dr. Dudley, rubbing his hands together. "No expense is too great at times such as these."

He pulled aside the rest of the canvas tarp.

"Hey! Those look like cross-country skis," said Drew, running his hand along the swooping tips. "I'd love to learn how to ski."

"So would I," said Annie, beginning to feel excited about it all, too.

"I've hired them for a week's time; that should be long enough."

Mr. Pipes pulled off his wool hat and scratched his bald crown. Then he challenged, "My dear fellow, this article states clearly that the storm is not due to strike for *two more days!*"

"Ah, that is where my foresight comes into clearer focus, isn't it," said Dr. Dudley. "One would be most unwise, my learned friend, to wait until Thursday to prepare for a storm hitting on Thursday, now, wouldn't he? Here, now, let me help you into the pickup."

As the engine warmed, Mr. Pipes ventured to say, "My dear Dr. Dudley, have you forgotten that we must fly to California tomorrow—twenty-four hours before the storm is due to hit. We only have but one more day after today."

Drew groaned, and Annie felt torn by it all. A snowstorm would be so fun, but what about Mr. Pipes witnessing to their parents?

"I knew we'd miss it," said Drew.

Dr. Dudley did his codfish imitation—eyes wide with mouth opening and closing soundlessly.

"W-well!" he said at last. "The timing of the forecast must simply be incorrect."

Lord, with Glowing Heart I'd Praise Thee

*To the praise of his glorious grace, which he has freely given us in the
One he loves.* Eph. 1:6

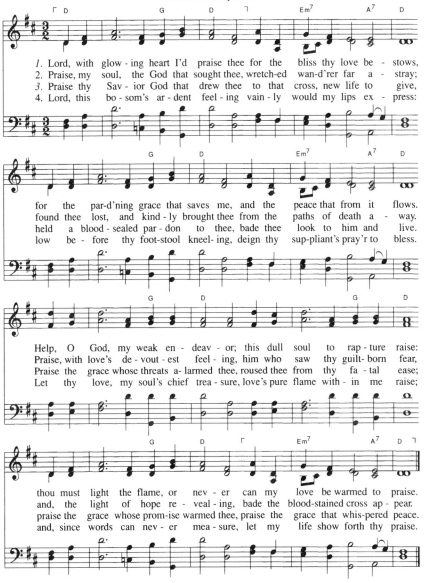

1. Lord, with glow-ing heart I'd praise thee for the bliss thy love be - stows,
2. Praise, my soul, the God that sought thee, wretch-ed wan-d'rer far a - stray;
3. Praise thy Sav - ior God that drew thee to that cross, new life to give,
4. Lord, this bo - som's ar - dent feel-ing vain-ly would my lips ex - press:

for the par-d'ning grace that saves me, and the peace that from it flows.
found thee lost, and kind - ly brought thee from the paths of death a - way.
held a blood - sealed par - don to thee, bade thee look to him and live.
low be - fore thy foot-stool kneel-ing, deign thy sup-pliant's pray'r to bless.

Help, O God, my weak en - deav - or; this dull soul to rap - ture raise:
Praise, with love's de - vout - est feel - ing, him who saw thy guilt-born fear,
Praise the grace whose threats a - larmed thee, roused thee from thy fa - tal ease;
Let thy love, my soul's chief trea - sure, love's pure flame with - in me raise;

thou must light the flame, or nev - er can my love be warmed to praise.
and, the light of hope re - veal - ing, bade the blood-stained cross ap - pear.
praise the grace whose prom-ise warmed thee, praise the grace that whis-pered peace.
and, since words can nev - er mea - sure, let my life show forth thy praise.

Francis Scott Key, 1817

RIPLEY 8.7.8.7.D.
Gregorian chant
Arr. by Lowell Mason, 1839

Chapter Six

Phillips Brooks
1835-1893

O holy Child of Bethlehem,
Descend to us, we pray;
Cast out our sin, and enter in,
Be born in us today.

Dr. Dudley held the driver's side door open and gestured for them to get in. Annie and Drew suppressed giggles as they and Mr. Pipes squeezed past the steering wheel, getting into the cab. Dr. Dudley slammed the door and fairly pranced in anticipation to the passenger side of the truck.

"Oh, the dear fellow has forgotten on which side you drive," observed Mr. Pipes.

Dr. Dudley opened the passenger door and abruptly halted, blinking rapidly, his eyes searching for the steering wheel.

"We thank you, my friend," said Mr. Pipes, nodding his head toward the steering wheel on the other side of the cab, "for checking on us; all is well."

Dr. Dudley stood there, holding the open door, his moustache twitching. Annie and Drew felt like bursting.

"Yes, well. Right, then," he said after a moment. They all sat wordlessly, as Dr. Dudley, slightly ruffled, came back around to the drivers seat and started the engine.

Mr. Pipes gave Dr. Dudley directions to an old Boston restaurant for lunch. As they halted in front of the four-story brick building, Drew read the sign:

"Ye olde Onion Oyster House, established, 1826. Ladies and Gents Sea Grill.' That's pretty old."

"Annie, my dear," said Mr. Pipes, looking at Annie's worried expression. "They have many other things to eat in addition to seafood, though you might enjoy a bowl of clam chowder—New England style."

"I-I'll try a bowl if you think so," said Annie with a grimace.

Several minutes later, the waiter set steaming bowls of creamy clam chowder on their table, dusted his hands and said, "D'ya want cwackers?"

All four stared dumbly at the waiter, who repeated impatiently, "D'ya want cwackers?"

Mr. Pipes cleared his throat and said, "I am most awfully sorry, dear fellow, but I do not understand your question. Perhaps, if you—"

"I'm speakin' plain Eenglish—D'ya want cwackers, for cwying out loud?"

"I get it!" Drew burst out, "*R*'s are *W*'s here. Yes, please, I love crackers crunched up in my soup."

"Good save, dear boy," said Dr. Dudley, when the waiter left. "But, mind you, if that man was speaking plain English, then I must be speaking ancient Abyssinian!"

Moments later Annie stared doubtfully at her bowl. She looked out the window at the gray sky; Christmas shoppers walked by, bundled and braced against the chilly winds. It was definitely another soup day, she thought. And after crunching three packages of crackers into the soup, she brought the spoon cautiously to her lips.

Drew finished his bowl and, looking around hungrily, asked if he could have a second one. Annie took another bite.

"What do you think, my dear?" asked Mr. Pipes.

"I actually like everything about it," replied Annie, "except those chewy little bits I get every now and then. Other than that, it's great."

After they finished eating, Mr. Pipes spread his map of New England on the table and said, "We are presently here, in Boston. And I propose we take Dr. Dudley's pickup north along the motorway I-95," he traced the route with his index finger, "to the town of Amesbury, just here."

"That's right on the border of Massachusetts," said Drew, "and New Hampster."

"*Hampshire*, I believe it is called," said Dr. Dudley, "a name of *English* origin."

"What's there?" asked Annie.

"Oh, it is a lovely rural New England village," replied Mr. Pipes. "And one of your somewhat unlikely hymn writers lived there for much of his life. It is not so far away that we cannot get there and back to Boston before our flight tomorrow."

"And miss Dr. Dudley's snow storm," said Drew heavily.

"I am afraid we must," said Mr. Pipes.

Annie breathed a sigh mixed with relief and disappointment.

❖ ❖ ❖

While driving through Boston, Drew caught sight of an impressive old building.

"Hey, that church reminds me of the really old cathedrals we saw on the Rhine River last summer."

Dr. Dudley stopped at a red traffic light, and they all looked at the church.

"That is Trinity Church," said Mr. Pipes. "American Romanesque, and you are correct, Drew; it is built along the lines of those ancient churches in Europe."

"Who is the man raising his arm in the statue?" asked Annie.

"Ah, that is Phillips Brooks, the Bishop of Boston," replied Mr. Pipes. "He was a bishop in the Episcopal Church, which is very much related to our Anglican Church in England."

"Why did he get a statue?" asked Drew.

The light turned green and Dr. Dudley drove on.

"Well, he was a most loved minister of the true gospel of Jesus Christ in a day—alas, like today—when most ministers preached froth—moralizing sentiment instead of the liberating message of sin and forgiveness through Christ. His church grew under his faithful care, and they eventually built that lovely structure in which to worship God."

Drew stole a last look at the towers and arches of the church before they turned a corner.

"Reverend Brooks, who never married, was known all over Boston for his thoughtful biblical preaching, his tenderness and sweetness, and especially for his love of children."

"Tell us more about him," said Annie.

"The story goes that on an April Fool's Day, Mr. Brooks strode down the street near the Public Garden and caught sight of a young boy straining to reach a doorbell. Brooks halted and, reaching for the bell pull, said kindly, 'Let me help you, my little man!' When the doorbell gonged, the boy tore down the steps yelling over his shoulder, 'Now run like the devil!'"

"Rotter!" said Dr. Dudley. "I've had that little monster's sort pull the same stunt at my door."

Mr. Pipes glanced at Drew and thought he detected a look of guilt in his diverted eyes.

"Do you think the people were mad at Reverend Brooks when they opened the door?" asked Annie.

"I suspect," said Mr. Pipes, "that he quickly turned it into a pastoral call. But he may have had a different sort of pastoral conversation the next time he saw that little boy."

"Little imp deserved a good tongue lashing," said Dr. Dudley.

"Now, Annie," continued Mr. Pipes, "you will be pleased to know that Reverend Brooks wrote poetry—especially carols. And I suspect you already know one of his Christmas carols."

"Which one is it?" asked Annie.

"I'll tell you how he wrote it," said Mr. Pipes, "and we shall see if you can guess."

"Okay," said Annie and Drew together.

"In the winter of 1865," began Mr. Pipes, "your devastating Civil War finally ended and Reverend Brooks made a pilgrimage to Palestine. The day before Christmas, he rode on horseback from Jerusalem to Bethlehem, visiting the place where Christ came to bring peace on earth. As the sun began to set, he rode east out of Bethlehem to the field where tradition tells us the shepherds watched their flocks by night and where the angels announced Christ's birth."

"'While Shepherds Watch Their Flocks by Night'? Is that it?" asked Drew.

"No."

"Well, it wouldn't be 'Hark! the Herald Angels Sing,'" said Annie. "That's Mr. Wesley's."

"Shall I continue?" said Mr. Pipes, smiling at them.

"Yes," they chimed in.

"With wonder he gazed at the 'shepherds keeping watch over their flocks by night,' as those blessed shepherds must have done 2,000 years ago. And he looked out over the dark village, the silent stars twinkling over the little town of Bethlehem—"

"'O Little Town of Bethlehem'!" said Drew. "That's it!"

"Right you are, my boy," said Mr. Pipes. "Mr. Brooks rode back to the town and celebrated Christmas in Constantine's ancient basilica, built in A.D. 326 over the traditional site of the stable cave where Mary gave birth to the baby Jesus. It was a long and thrilling service. When he returned to America he wrote 'O Little Town of Bethlehem' for the children in his Sunday School. His organist, Lewis Redner, composed the music for this much-loved Christmas carol, included in nearly every hymnal and sung the world over."

"Can we sing it?" asked Annie.

"Most certainly," said Mr. Pipes. "Do notice how Reverend Brooks poetically speaks to Bethlehem in the first verse, to the stars in the second, and finally to the 'Holy Child of Bethlehem' in the last. The third verse, and the one most frequently omitted, is particularly important for explaining how God mysteriously 'imparts to hu-

man hearts' through Christ, salvation from our 'world of sin.'"

He gave them the note, and the cab of the pickup rang with Christmas cheer:

O little town of Bethlehem,
How still we see thee lie;
Above thy deep and dreamless sleep
The silent stars go by:
Yet in thy dark streets shineth
The everlasting Light;
The hopes and fears of all the years
Are met in thee tonight.

For Christ is born of Mary;
And gathered all above,
While mortals sleep, the angels keep
Their watch of wond'ring love.
O morning stars, together
Proclaim the holy birth;
And praises sing to God the King,
And peace to men on earth.

How silently, how silently
The wondrous gift is giv'n!
So God imparts to human hearts
The blessings of his heav'n.
No ear may hear his coming,
But in this world of sin,
Where meek souls will receive him still,
The dear Christ enters in.

O Holy Child of Bethlehem,
Descend to us, we pray;
Cast out our sin, and enter in,
Be born in us today.
We hear the Christmas angels
The great glad tidings tell;
O come to us, abide with us,
Our Lord Emmanuel.

When they finished the carol Dr. Dudley leaned forward, looked at the gray sky, and turned up the heater.

"It has a sort of sweetness to it," said Annie, holding her hands over the warm air coming from the vent on the dash. "Like he wrote it especially for children."

"Yes," agreed Mr. Pipes. "One cannot sing it without hearing something of Reverend Brooks's love of little children in it."

"I like the way being there," said Drew, "you know, in Bethlehem, inspired him to write it. It's kind of like Mr. Key writing on the ship during the battle."

Annie twisted a lock of her blond hair around her finger. Maybe that was why she couldn't think of a good poem to write for a hymn: she didn't have any great experiences like Mr. Brooks or Mr. Key.

"Oh, but of course," said Mr. Pipes, almost as if reading Annie's mind, "there are many great hymns—perhaps most of them—written very methodically without any inspiring circumstance beyond a deep appreciation of God and the grand truths of his Word.

"In any case, Phillips Brooks lives on and is remembered best for this carol. He died in 1893, and when one of the children in his parish heard from her mother that Reverend Brooks had died, the five-year-old girl exclaimed, 'Oh, mama, how happy the angels will be!'"

"That was a pretty grown-up way of looking at his death," said Annie.

They all agreed, and for several miles, Mr. Pipes led them in singing as many other Christmas carols as they could remember. Dr. Dudley joined in, heartily beating time on the steering wheel. They finished with Isaac Watts's 'Joy to the World'!"

"Didn't you tell us that Watts' carol was a Psalm versification?" asked Annie.

"Yes, I believe I did," said Mr. Pipes. "Isaac Watts found the material to write this grand carol from Psalm 98. If you, my dear, have never stood on the decks of a ship in a great battle or gazed on the fields where angels proclaimed Jesus' birth, go to the

Psalms. Find one whose prayer and praise especially gives words to your own longings after God, then make that Psalm yours by writing its message in rhyme and meter."

Annie thumbed to the Psalms in her pocket Bible.

"'Amesbury, three miles,'" read Drew on a road sign. "Our turnoff's just ahead."

"We must find a call box, Dr. Dudley," said Mr. Pipes. "I have here a telephone number for the Whittier House, open in winter by appointment only. It says to ring for an appointment."

Dr. Dudley broke into a smug grin and began, "Therein you will see more of my foresight—" He was cut off by a sort of muffled warbling inside his jacket. Looking startled, he groped at his chest. "Am I—Am I having a h—"

"What's that!" said Drew. "Have you got some kind of bird inside your jacket?"

A wave of understanding came over Dr. Dudley and he pulled a small black cellular phone from his pocket. It warbled louder.

"How do I answer the dashed thing?" he demanded, poking at the buttons.

Drew took the phone from him. "I never thought *you* would get a cell phone, Dr. Dudley," he said, pushing the "talk" key and handing the phone back to Dr. Dudley.

"The article suggested a cellular phone for the storm. Bother! What do I do next?" said Dr. Dudley, scowling at the phone.

"Say 'hello,'" said Drew.

"Hello," said Dr. Dudley. Then holding the phone away from his mouth, "This is rather exciting; my first call with it—but whoever could it be? I do hope Mrs. Broadwith's rheumatism isn't acting up; precious little I can do from here."

He listened quietly for a moment.

"Do mind the road, dear man," said Mr. Pipes. "Things are getting a bit icy. Slow and steady, our exit lies just ahead—to the *right*."

Dr. Dudley frowned and said into the phone: "Vinyl what?" He again held the phone aside and said, "Do any of you need— vinyl siding—or windows? Ah, and how very considerate: chap says he'll have someone in our neighborhood especially to inspect our dwelling. What do you think?"

Annie and Drew burst out laughing. "Dr. Dudley," gasped Annie at last, "it's a phone solicitation—you know, a salesman on the phone."

"But I never asked anyone to call," said Dr. Dudley.

"In America," said Annie, "they just call anyway. Be glad we aren't eating dinner."

"Tell him," said Drew, "that your house is 300 years old, made of stone, with leaded windows—and that it's 3,000 miles away. That should do it."

O Little Town of Bethlehem

Bethlehem Ephrathah, though you are small ... out of you will come for me one who will be ruler over Israel, whose origins are from of old, from ancient times. Mic. 5:2

1. O lit-tle town of Beth-le-hem, how still we see thee lie;
2. For Christ is born of Mar-y; and gath-ered all a-bove,
3. How si-lent-ly, how si-lent-ly, the won-drous gift is giv'n!
4. O ho-ly child of Beth-le-hem, de-scend to us, we pray;

a-bove thy deep and dream-less sleep the si-lent stars go by:
while mor-tals sleep, the an-gels keep their watch of won-d'ring love.
So God im-parts to hu-man hearts the bless-ings of his heav'n.
cast out our sin and en-ter in; be born in us to-day.

yet in thy dark streets shin-eth the ev-er-last-ing Light;
O morn-ing stars, to-geth-er pro-claim the ho-ly birth!
No ear may hear his com-ing, but in this world of sin,
We hear the Christ-mas an-gels the great glad tid-ings tell;

the hopes and fears of all the years are met in thee to-night.
And prais-es sing to God the King, and peace to men on earth.
where meek souls will re-ceive him still, the dear Christ en-ters in.
O come to us, a-bide with us, our Lord Em-man-u-el.

Phillips Brooks, 1868

ST. LOUIS C.M.D.irreg.
Lewis H. Redner, 1868

Chapter Seven

John Greenleaf Whittier
1807-1892

> I find my old accustomed place among
> My brethren, where, perchance, no human tongue
> Shall utter words: where never hymn is sung,
> Nor deep-toned organ blown, nor censor swung.

After Mr. Pipes phoned the woman who took care of the Whittier House, they continued off the interstate, following her directions.

"Lovely little place," said Dr. Dudley, as they drove down Main Street.

"All right, then" said Mr. Pipes, reading the directions. "'Follow Main Street to Market Square'—ah, yes, this looks like Market Square. 'Go around the rotary until you face back the way you came.'"

"Whatever is a 'rotary'?" asked Dr. Dudley.

"From the looks of that—just there," said Mr. Pipes, pointing forward. "I should think it is the same as a roundabout—No, no, counterclockwise, my dear man! Then, the directions say, 'look for the fork with a sign to the Whittier House.'"

Amesbury appeared to be made up largely of late nineteenth-century brick mill buildings converted into shops, offices, and even homes. Friends Street veered to the left past a three-story brick building wedged in the fork. Sooner than any of them expected, Mr. Pipes said, "86 Friends Street—this is it." And Dr. Dudley stopped the pickup before a tidy but rather plain-looking white house. It sat solid but unadorned on a low hill above the road, a wide chimney rose from the center of the roofline. Flanking the house, tangled branches of a leafless hawthorn tree creaked stiffly in the wind, and fir trees rising from behind hissed and swayed against a cold gray sky.

"Bur-r-r, humbug!" said Drew, zipping up his jacket as he stepped out of the truck and mounted the stairs. A low stone wall lined the matted grass of the unfenced front yard. "We're way out in the middle of No-wheres-ville, that's for sure."

Tears rose in Mr. Pipes's eyes, and he blinked rapidly in the icy wind as he glanced nervously up at the thickening clouds.

A woman—wearing a thick wool sweater with reindeer on it, Levis, and fleecy slippers—met them at the six-panel front door.

"You've picked a cold one," she said. "Welcome to The Whittier House. My husband and I are the caretakers. Come on in."

Annie immediately liked the house as they stepped into the narrow entry hall. She smiled at the interlocking flower patterns on the wallpaper. Split maple logs snapped in a fireplace to their left. Dr. Dudley pulled off his gloves with his teeth and warmed his hands; the others joined him.

"I say," he said. "Who would have believed one could become so cold from the pickup to the house. A lovely fire, madam, and most inviting."

The caretaker led them throughout the simple rooms, explaining that all the furnishings—the chairs, tables, beds, dishes, hats, even the wallpaper—were here when John Greenleaf Whittier, the Quaker poet and abolitionist, lived for fifty-six years within these walls. She showed them a display of actual quill pens Mr. Whittier used to write his poetry.

Annie decided that there was something charming about the polished floors, the rows of books, and the functional simplicity of the old house.

"Whittier liked the 'venerable dead,' too," said Drew, nodding toward the books lining one wall of the kitchen.

"Yes, it appears that he did," said Mr. Pipes.

"Oh, look at the hand pump for water,' said Annie.

"Try it," said the caretaker.

Annie lifted the handle up and down and a stream of water fell into the porcelain sink. She ran her finger through the water.

"Ouch!" she squealed. "It feels like ice!"

In the parlor, Drew crossed the room and stared into a glass case at a life-size white face. He pressed his face against the glass for a better look.

"What's this?" he asked.

"Oh, that old thing," said the caretaker with a light laugh. "That's Whittier's death mask."

Drew jumped back.

"Death mask?" stammered Annie in horror.

"They often did that with famous people in the old days," explained the caretaker. "They took a plaster cast of his face in 1892 right after he died—I suppose that way no one would forget what he looked like."

Annie studied a portrait of Mr. Whittier hanging on the wall. His cockeyed smile, dark eyes and protruding white beard made him look, she thought, kind of severe.

"So what did he do that made people want to remember him?" asked Drew, glancing back at the cabinet, "with a death mask?"

"Well, for starters, he became America's second most famous poet in his own lifetime," said the caretaker. "Next, of course to Longfellow," she added as if she didn't quite agree with history. "He was so famous that this house has been kept as a museum in his honor since soon after his passing. He is loved for his poems about nature, history, slavery, and religion."

"Tell us one of them?" asked Annie.

"Well, he's best known for his poem, 'Snowbound,'" she answered, "written in his Garden Room, where he wrote most all his poetry—follow me; I'll show you it."

Mr. Pipes followed and went immediately to the tall window overlooking the back yard. He looked nervously out at the massive old maple tree, its stiff black branches extending protectively over the yard. His brow furrowed as he squinted at the black trunk. Was that a snowflake slanting before the wind in front of it? Hmm, he couldn't be sure. But it was getting colder, and the last thing he wanted was to get caught out in a storm on the high-way back to Boston—Dr. Dudley's sleeping bags or not.

"So he wrote 'Snowbound' right here?" Mr. Pipes heard Drew ask.

"How does it go?" asked Annie, moving to Mr. Pipes's side at the window.

"Oh, it's terribly long," laughed the caretaker, glancing out the window, "like our winter storms can be sometimes."

Mr. Pipes turned and looked anxiously at the caretaker.

She went on. "It's been an unusually mild winter this year—so far. Whittier particularly hated snow and wrote Snow-bound—no doubt, looking with distaste out this same win-dow—during one long cold blizzard that kept him inside longer than he liked. But I might remember a few lines of it." She looked again out the window and frowned.

"Let me see, it goes:

> Arrives the snow, and, driving o're the fields—
> The sled and traveler stopped …
> Delayed … the housemates sit
> Around the radiant fireplace—

"No, no, no, I'm sorry," she interrupted herself, "that's Emerson. Ah, here it is." She pulled a leather volume from the shelf and read:

> The sun that brief December day
> Rose cheerless over hills of gray …
> Slow tracing down the thickening sky
> Its mute and ominous prophecy …
> A chill no coat, however stout,
> Of homespun stuff could quite shut out,
> A hard, dull bitterness of cold,
> That checked, mid-vein, the circling race
> Of life-blood in the sharpened face,
> The coming of the snowstorm told …

Mr. Pipes shuddered.

"He's good," said Annie, when the caretaker stopped.

"And he, no doubt," said Dr. Dudley, looking hopefully out the window at the clouds, his hands clasped behind his back, and lifting himself up and down on his toes as he spoke, "would have had a thing or two to say about today's weather—and the forecast."

"Indeed," said Mr. Pipes, looking though the shrubbery of his eyebrows at the cold yard. "Remembering, of course, that Mr. Whittier quite wisely did not take pleasure in snowstorms—nor should we, under present circumstances."

Annie bit her lip and looked around the cozy garden room, its fire glowing warmly, and at the desk where Mr. Whittier wrote his poetry. Maybe a snowstorm could inspire her like it did him. But then, they'd miss Christmas with their parents, and worse yet, their parents would miss getting to know Mr. Pipes better. She sighed, a frustrated all-at-once sigh.

"Well, Mr. Whittier must have written hymns," said Drew, to Mr. Pipes. "Or you wouldn't have brought us all the way up here to see his house."

"Hymns? Heavens, no," said the caretaker. "He was a Quaker."

Puzzled, Annie and Drew looked at their old friend.

"What's a Quaker believe?" asked Annie.

"Oh, Quakers didn't go in for traditional religious creeds and services," continued the caretaker. "They believed we each have an inner light—you know, truth from within. So Quakers met on First Day as equals and composed their spirits in silence, waiting, I guess, for the inner spark of divinity to ignite. There was no preacher, of course no liturgy or order of worship. And he couldn't have written hymns—I'm sure of it—because Quakers didn't sing hymns."

"So, no singing in church—ever?" asked Annie.

"No organs?" asked Drew.

"No music of any kind—ever," said the caretaker. "He even wrote poems against hymns and organs and such things. Fact is, in many of the services over the centuries at the Meeting House just down the road, people gathered and sat in total silence, not even speaking, let alone singing, start to finish for the whole meeting. No, no, definitely no hymns written here."

Annie looked up at Mr. Pipes; had he made a mistake about Whittier? She reached up and gently touched his sleeve. "It's okay," she whispered consolingly in his ear, "I like the house anyway."

Mr. Pipes patted her hand and smiled.

The caretaker went on to tell all about Whittier's concern for ending slavery in America, his political activism for the abolition of slavery, his service in the Massachusetts legislature, and his contribution to founding the Republican Party. When she finished, she invited them to stay for a cup of tea; Dr. Dudley and the children were about to eagerly accept when Mr. Pipes said:

"No, thank you ever so much. But, I am afraid it is simply out of the question, under the circumstances." He glanced out a nearby window. "We must be underway to Boston immediately. Perhaps you were correct, Dr. Dudley. The storm has arrived early and there is, I fear, no time to lose."

"Now just you wait," said Dr. Dudley curtly. "We have come all this way only to turn around and race back to Boston, have we? Humph, not if I have anything to say about it. And considering the fact that I am driving the pickup, I flatter myself in saying I most certainly *do* have something to say about it. There, I've said it."

Annie and Drew looked from Dr. Dudley to Mr. Pipes. Surely he's not upset because it turns out in the end Whittier didn't have anything to do with hymns, thought Drew. That just wouldn't be like Mr. Pipes, would it?

"Mr. Pipes," ventured Drew. "You did say the storm wasn't going to hit until Friday. We have time to look around a little more before then."

Mr. Pipes pulled aside a curtain and peeked again at the clouds. He flexed his fingers.

"You do remember my joints?" said Mr. Pipes. "They are now speaking quite clearly about this storm. Oh, I have no intention of being the delayed travelers mentioned in Emerson's poem." He ran his hand through his white hair. "And I am mortally certain that those are snowflakes out there."

With squeals, both Annie and Drew bolted to the window.

Mr. Pipes went on: "We do have obligations—airline tickets for example, and your parents' expectation of our arrival tomorrow. No, we must take no risks with getting snowbound in some hotel along the highway—or worse—and missing our flight. Every argument compels me to insist that we be away—now! Naturally we are most grateful for your time," he continued to the caretaker. "And the offer of tea, but you do understand my concerns."

"Sure do," said the caretaker. "I'd a never left Boston with this forecast."

"Oh, then we must away!" said Mr. Pipes, herding them to the door and helping Annie put her coat on.

"I'm half tempted to suggest," said Dr. Dudley, narrowing his eyes at the old man. "That you, Mr. Pipes, are somewhat out of sorts about something."

"Indeed!" said Mr. Pipes. "The weather! And our safe and timely arrival in California."

Bracing against the icy wind and the pinprick searing of a swirling snowflake driven hard against the cheek, they ran to the pickup and scrambled in. Dr. Dudley fidgeted with the keys.

"Please, Dr. Dudley," said Mr. Pipes after a moment's silence, "do start the engine—I fear we are in for a treacherous drive to Boston, and we've no time to waste."

"I am *trying* to start the engine," snapped Dr. Dudley, icily. "But when I turn the key, like this, nothing—mind you—*nothing* happens."

Mr. Pipes groaned. Annie and Drew couldn't help looking at each other in wide-eyed excitement.

"Do try again," urged Mr. Pipes.

"Funny thing with frozen gas lines," said Dr. Dudley, looking soberly at the instrument panel, "Try though one might, in this cold, they remain quite stubbornly—frozen."

"Frozen, you say?" said Mr. Pipes.

"Like ice," replied Dr. Dudley, looking at his friend with a look that suggested he may have just gotten more than he bargained for.

No one spoke for a full minute.

"Cool!" blurted Drew, at last.

Mr. Pipes stared hard at him.

"Look!" said Annie, pointing back at the house. "The caretaker is signaling at the front door."

Mr. Pipes opened the passenger door.

"I've just listened to the weather on the radio," she called. "You are advised not to leave home except in an emergency. The storm's here, and it looks like a biggy."

Annie gripped Drew's arm.

"Cool!" he said, again.

"We have already left home, I fear," called Mr. Pipes. "There can be nothing for it but to get to Boston."

"Good luck," called the caretaker. "But I'd never try it—not with children."

"What are we to do?" Mr. Pipes murmured to himself.

"Get your things, and come back inside," the caretaker's voice rose and fell with the wind.

It took a frigid half hour to unload all Dr. Dudley's supplies—food in the kitchen, sleeping bags, and extra clothing in bedrooms, and cross-country skis against the wall in the Garden Room. When they finished, the caretaker said:

"My husband and I live in the attached caretaker's quarters." She paused, looking at the cases of canned goods. "It looks like you have plenty of food—in fact, I'd say you look well prepared for a New England snowstorm."

Dr. Dudley drew himself up to his full height, his chin aloft.

"Firewood's in the summer kitchen," she went on. And then laughing brightly she added, "And you're snowbound in Whittier's own house. Well, be careful of the china and holler if you need anything." And she was gone.

"Cool!" said Drew. "This is so cool!"

◈ ◈ ◈

"But it's seventy-five degrees here." Mr. Pipes held Dr. Dudley's cellular phone awkwardly as he listened to Annie and Drew's mother on the other end. "Really, Mr. Pipes, I totally can't imagine a storm, you know, like you're describing. You sure this isn't another one of Drew's tricks?"

"I assure you, madam," said Mr. Pipes, looking out the window at driving snow. "We are delayed beyond hope of getting to the airport in Boston—any time soon."

"Well, then, when?" asked their mother.

"I cannot say," replied Mr. Pipes. "Perhaps only hours," he said doubtfully, "but I am inclined to think it something more like days—perhaps more. Oh, I really have no idea, and I am most awfully sorry for this. I only wish there was something anyone could do. But, madam, we are so clearly in the hands of Providence in the weather, as in all things—especially obvious in *this* weather. I can only assure you that the children will be most carefully guarded and cared for and that we will away to Boston at the very first possibility of success in getting there safely."

Mr. Pipes gave Annie and Drew the phone and they wished their mother a Merry Christmas; their stepfather was away on business, but she expected him home by Christmas Eve—Saturday.

Dr. Dudley gave Mr. Pipes an I-told-you-so look and said, "There's simply nothing for it but to make the most of it. I've planned it all out, perfectly, if I do say so myself. We have plenty of stores, and I for one intend to organize our situation and prepare dinner. With a heavy sigh, Mr. Pipes joined him in the kitchen.

Excited as she felt sitting on a braided rug in front of the crackling fire in the little kitchen, Annie felt a wave of longing—not really homesickness—but a longing for her parents to sit and listen to Mr. Pipes, to sip tea with him, to ask him questions, to believe in Mr. Pipes's God.

"Wouldn't it be great," she said, after saying good-bye and turning the phone off, "If Mom and Dad could come here?"

Mr. Pipes smiled at her as the teakettle began whistling. "It is a great pity, my dear, that we are not with them at holiday time." He handed her the plates and silverware, and she began setting four places at the old trestle table for dinner.

Drew peered out a frosty window, snow pelting in gusty waves against it, at the gathering storm and the fading light of the short winter day. The red pickup rapidly glazed over with snow. He smiled. It looked like frosting on a truck-shaped birthday cake—which reminded him. He sniffed. Umm, something smelled awfully good!

"Anything I can do to help," he said, rejoining the others in the kitchen.

"More wood on the fire, my boy," said Dr. Dudley. "Ah, I'll have this stew—labeled, 'Western Style Chili'—hotted and ready in a moment. Though new to my palate, smells good enough. Annie, dear, slice this loaf of bread—nice and thick, if you please—and spread each slice generously with butter. And, Drew, open this tin of applesauce; I'll hot it in a jiffy and we'll spread it on the bread."

Mr. Pipes emptied the contents of two cans of creamy corn into a saucepan and stirred it over the iron top of the kitchen stove.

"We gonna have *cwackers* with our chili?" asked Drew, laughing.

"Oh, and cheese melted on top is awfully good," said Annie.

Dr. Dudley gave Annie a wooden cutting board and she sat at the table slicing cheese as thinly as she could.

When all was ready the foursome sat around Whittier's kitchen table and Mr. Pipes led in prayer.

"Oh Lord," he began, that reverent familiarity in his voice that always made Drew think Mr. Pipes was talking directly with God. "The God Who 'covers the sky with clouds, Who sends His command to the earth and spreads the snow like wool and scatters the frost like ashes; who can withstand Your icy blasts…?'"

As he continued, Annie mused at his prayer. It sounded like a Psalm; Mr. Pipes even prayed the Psalter, she decided.

Darkness had fallen when they finished eating. They chatted companionably as they heated up water drawn from the hand pump and washed up the dishes. Annie and Drew frequently bolted with squeals of delight to the window and cupping their hands against the frozen windowpane, peered at the growing whiteness outside.

Mr. Pipes and Annie made another pot of tea while Dr. Dudley and Drew lit candles in the Garden Room. They scooted four cane chairs up close to the warm glow of the fireplace. Munching cookies and sipping tea, they warmed their toes before the fire and listened to the wind whistling in the eaves and creaking in the snow-laden, old maple tree outside. Snowflakes stuttered in an icy staccato against the windowpanes. Annie shivered, not so much from cold as from the cozy excitement of it all.

"This is so much fun," said Drew. "And it's okay if Mr. Whittier didn't write any hymns, Mr. Pipes. We're awfully glad you brought us here."

"Mr. Pipes," said Annie, warming her hands on her tea mug as she gazed into the fire. "Was the caretaker right about Mr. Whittier not liking hymns because he was a Quaker?"

The rubbed and polished old turnings of Mr. Whittier's rocking chair creaked rhythmically as Mr. Pipes rocked back and forth.

"It is somewhat confusing with Mr. Whittier," he began. "On the one hand he most certainly did disparage hymns and organs and the like used in worship."

He pulled a volume of Whittier poetry off the shelf and skimmed down the table of contents

"Ah, here it is:

> I find my old accustomed place among
> My brethren, where, perchance, no human tongue

Shall utter words: where never hymn is sung,
Nor deep-toned organ blown, nor censor swung.

"He wrote often about his ideal of the Quaker meeting, devoid of any spiritual ritual but silence."

"Sounds like a guy who would never write a hymn, then," said Drew.

"That is where the confusion comes in," said Mr. Pipes. "Mr. Whittier seemed to not value hymns, but at the same time stated 'A good hymn is the best use to which poetry can be devoted.' He went on to say that in writing his poetry he never successfully reached poetry's best use—the hymn."

"Too bad," said Annie.

"Ah, but I do not agree with him," said Mr. Pipes, leaning forward in his chair.

"About what?" asked Drew.

"Writing a hymn," said Mr. Pipes. "Though, in much of his poetry, Whittier seems more devoted to the praise of abolitionism than to the praise of God; he did, however, write at least one poem worthy to be mentioned here."

"Do you think he wrote it," asked Annie, "right here—in this room?"

"I suspect he did," replied Mr. Pipes, looking around the room. "It goes like this:

All things are Thine; no gift have we,
Lord of all gifts, to offer Thee;
And hence with grateful hearts today,
Thine own before Thy feet we lay.

"'Thine own before Thy feet we lay,'" repeated Annie. "These words remind us not to be proud when giving to God—after all, God gave everything to us in the first place."

"Yes, indeed," replied Mr. Pipes.

"How does the rest of it go?" asked Drew.

"One moment, please." After rummaging through the bookcase, Mr. Pipes found the hymn in two volumes of Whittier's poetry and handed them to Annie, Drew, and Dr. Dudley.

"Follow along," said Mr. Pipes. "Drew, you will no doubt enjoy J. S. Bach's arrangement of the thoughtful tune, 'Pensum Sacrum,' to which it is set."

He hummed the dignified melody, and when he finished they joined him:

> Thy will was in the builders' thought;
> Thy hand unseen amidst us wrought;
> Through mortal motive, scheme and plan,
> Thy wise eternal purpose ran.
>
> In weakness and in want we call
> On Thee for whom the heavens are small;
> Thy glory is Thy children's good,
> Thy joy Thy tender Fatherhood.

Mr. Pipes paused. "This last verse—a prayer of petition to God—is most appropriate for us to pray when we enter God's House to worship Him."

> O Father, deign these walls to bless;
> Fill with Thy love their emptiness;
> And let their door a gateway be
> To lead us from ourselves to Thee.

His face glowing orange from the hot coals, Drew positioned another split maple log on the fire; it crackled eagerly, sparks rising into the chimney.

"I-I like it," said Annie hesitantly.

"But it is kind of different," said Drew, "from Mr. Key and the others' hymns—I'm not quite sure what's missing."

"Sin," said Annie, after a moment.

"What?" exclaimed Dr. Dudley.

"Sin, that's what's missing," she explained.

"Yeah," said Drew. "Nothing here about pardon or forgiveness."

"Full marks, my dears!" said Mr. Pipes, smiling at them. "Whittier, alas, had little sense of sin and thus of man's great need of grace—themes explored in most Psalms and hymns historically sung by the church. Most, though not all great hymns, include these themes, mind you, but you will be hard pressed to find these truths celebrated in any of Whittier's religious poetry."

"So, was he a Christian?" asked Annie, "a real one?"

"I do not know his heart, my dear," said Mr. Pipes. "The Bible, however, is quite clear: Christ came to call sinners to repentance. If someone refuses to admit he is a sinner, that he is truly lost, whatever else he might say about Christ, he is not calling him Savior if he does not, in fact, believe he needs one."

"So, you can't be saved," said Annie, "unless you're lost—unless you know you're lost."

"Precisely," agreed Mr. Pipes. "But though we have good reason to scratch our heads at Whittier's profession, nevertheless, Whittier's hymn is another case of a bad theologian at his best when writing a hymn. In spite of disturbing doctrinal flaws in these lines, Whittier adorns the biblical and Reformation truth of how God providentially orders all events in the world for His glory and His children's good."

"He does it with that bit about the builder," said Drew, "right here." He pointed at the second verse of the poem.

> Thy will was in the builders' thought;
> Thy hand unseen amidst us wrought;
> Through mortal motive, scheme and plan,
> Thy wise eternal purpose ran.

"That reminds me of Anna Waring's line in her hymn," said Annie, "about all our lives being portioned out by God—so we don't have to fear the changes coming," she added slowly.

"It is the great confidence of the Christian," said Mr. Pipes, "that God is sovereign, and as the King of kings He brings about

His eternal purpose, perfectly guiding and governing all human plans, motives, and deeds."

They sat silently around the fire for several minutes, Annie and Drew thinking about these high mysteries.

"Oh, I say," said Dr. Dudley with a yawn, "I believe the storm will carry on without us."

"F-for how long, do you think?" asked Annie.

"That, my dear," replied Mr. Pipes, "is firmly in God's all-wise hands, and we needn't fear."

"Well, I for one," said Dr. Dudley, "am ready to retire."

"You're gonna quit being a doctor?" asked Drew.

Dr. Dudley rolled his eyes.

"Retire—as in, go to bed," he explained.

▨ ▨ ▨

Annie snuggled into her sleeping bag on one of Mr. Whittier's four-poster beds; her candle flickered on the bed stand, casting wobbly shadows on the wallpaper. Wind-driven, icy pebbles still chattered against the windowpanes and mingled with Drew's steady breathing coming from the trundle bed at her feet.

With a rustle of nylon sleeping bag, she leaned on her elbow and opened her Bible to the Psalms. Mr. Pipes had said to find a Psalm that sounded like her own prayer to God. She turned to Psalm 86 and read: "Hear, O Lord, and answer me, for I am poor and needy. Guard my life, for I am devoted to you. You are my God; save your servant.... I call to you all day long. Bring joy to your servant.... [Y]ou are great and do marvelous deeds.... Teach me your ways, O Lord, and I will walk in your truth; give me an undivided heart.... [Y]ou, O Lord, are a compassionate and gracious God.... Turn to me and have mercy on me; grant your strength to your servant.... [Y]ou, O Lord, have helped me and comforted me."

She breathed a deep longing sort of sigh and reached for her sketchbook. Running her eyes down the Psalm again, she bit her pencil for a moment then began writing:

> Great God, compassionate and kind,
> The God who hears my plea.
> You are my God whose name I fear;
> My Lord forever be.

Frowning, she scratched out two words in the last two lines. After rereading the last verses of the Psalm, she wrote:

> You are my *Strength* whose name I fear;
> My Help forever be.

All Things Are Thine

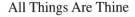

Everything comes from you, and we have given you only what comes from your hand. 1 Chron. 29:14

John G. Whittier, 1872

HERR JESU CHRIST L.M.
Pensum Sacrum, Görlitz, 1648
Arr. by Johann Sebastian Bach, 1685~1750

Chapter Eight

The Slave Spiritual and Southern Harmony

We'll run and never tire,
We'll run and never tire,
We'll run and never tire,
Jesus sets poor sinners free!

Next thing Annie knew, she awoke in a strange bedroom glowing with a dull white light from the window. Her sketchbook lay on the floor and her Bible lay next to her pillow.

"Drew?" Her breath made a little white cloud in the chill air. No answer. Breakfast smells drifted from the kitchen; of course Drew would be up. Steeling herself for the icy blast, she hopped out of the warm bed and, shivering, quickly dressed and went into the little kitchen.

"Okay, Dr. Dudley," she heard Drew saying, "If December twenty-fourth is Christmas Eve—this is a good one, now—what's December twenty-third?"

"Good morning, Annie," Mr. Pipes greeted her. "I trust you slept well, my dear?"

"I really don't remember anything about it," she laughed.

"That is a very good sign, indeed," he said. "Though its fury slackens, the storm is with us still—" He showed her out the kitchen window. "Snow falling apace and drifting high against the house in the winds. But we, though snowbound, are safe and warm inside, and you must refresh yourself with a hot cup of tea."

Mr. Pipes poured milk from a little white pitcher into her cup then added steaming tea. She thanked him, took the warm mug in both hands and closed her eyes, letting the tantalizing aroma engulf her face and warm her nose.

Dr. Dudley, wearing a green apron, greeted her from the stove, where he appeared to be frying bacon and boiling eggs.

"And if I may remind us all," he said, blinking and looking at the ceiling. "We are most thoroughly provisioned for said snowstorm."

"And we are most grateful, my friend," said Mr. Pipes generously.

"Anything I can do to help?" Annie asked Dr. Dudley, who put her to work opening a tin of peaches.

"Ah, excuse me," said Drew, sounding a little put out that his joke was interrupted. "So what is December twenty-third?"

"Let me see," said Mr. Pipes. "The day before Christmas Eve?"

Drew made a buzzer sound and shook his head.

"Thanks for playing; Dr. Dudley, what do you think?" he asked, grinning.

"The same as your Venerable Pipes."

"No, it's Christmas *Adam*! Get it? You know, if the twenty-fourth's Christmas Eve—"

"—I get it!" said Mr. Pipes, laughing heartily. Annie had heard the joke before, and Dr. Dudley only scratched his head. Drew slapped his palm on his knee and burst into laughter.

Mr. Pipes helped Annie set the table, while Drew worked at explaining the joke to Dr. Dudley.

"I observed candlelight," said Mr. Pipes softly to Annie, "under your door last night."

"I tried writing a poem," whispered Annie in her old friend's ear, "from a Psalm."

"Oh, I must see it soon." He smiled and winked at her.

For Dr. Dudley and Drew the conversation switched to food.

"Those aren't done," said Drew, looking at the pale bulges of greasy fat separated by hints of reddish meat in the strips of bacon.

"*Au contraire*, my boy," said Dr. Dudley, with a superior waggle of his head as he lifted another limp slice of bacon off the griddle onto the plate. "They are done to perfection: slid across the frying pan with minimal damage. That is the only way to prepare bacon, I assure you."

Drew frowned. "I like it crispy. You know, so it breaks off when you bite into it."

"Aha, we have a name for that, my dear boy," replied Dr. Dudley. "It's called burnt—burnt to a crisp. You've no doubt heard the phrase."

Dr. Dudley checked his watch. "Oh, three minutes is up; eggs are done."

"*Three minutes?*" said Drew. "That's all?"

"Oh, eggs, too, is it?" replied Dr. Dudley, steamily. "I suppose you want them hard and pithy inside—with all that luscious creaminess turned to concrete. Humph!"

"I just like my eggs and bacon cooked so there's no chance of any clucking or oinking while I'm eating," said Drew, looking wide-eyed as Dr. Dudley broke open an egg and checked the runny yoke with the tip of a teaspoon; yellow liquid dribbled back into the shell.

"Looks like the eggs are *undone*, to me," mumbled Drew.

"May I make so bold as to suggest," said Mr. Pipes, suppressing a smile, "there just might be room in this world for both opinions about eggs and bacon."

"Not whilst I do the cooking," said Dr. Dudley.

"How about if I give you a break," said Annie, who knew she could never choke down eggs and bacon cooked Dr. Dudley's way. "You just sit here by the fire and I'll finish cooking the rest of the eggs and bacon."

"Good work," whispered Drew in his sister's ear after they sat around the table and Mr. Pipes prayed. He peeled his eggs, munched them with the back of his fork and put a generous gob of butter on the mound. Melting butter dribbled through the eggs as he sprinkled salt and pepper on them and stirred crispy bits of bacon into the concoction. Dr. Dudley looked on in horror.

"That's why the bacon's got to be crispy," explained Drew. "Do you have any catsup? It'd be perfect topped with catsup!"

※ ※ ※

Later in the morning, Drew scraped the frosty inside of the window with his fingernails and peered out. Dr. Dudley's truck had grown into a small mountain of drifted snow. He felt a twinge of impatience: the storm would stop sometime, but then they'd have to leave because it was over and before he could get outside and really enjoy the snow. Sitting *inside* watching a snow-storm *outside* wasn't enough; he just had to get out in it. The wind still blew, but the snow fell in spurts and flurries. Mounds of drifted snow kept the doors firmly blocked. Drew paced from window to window.

Mr. Pipes, a book in hand, rocked in his chair before the fire. Dr. Dudley rustled and banged around in the kitchen, prying open a window to set out some food for birds or little creatures cut off from food by the snow. Annie helped him for a while then tucked her feet up and wrapped herself in a quilt in front of the fire. She opened a book of Whittier's anti-slavery poems and read silently:

> Shame! Shame!
> Still round our country's proudest hall
>   The trade in human flesh is driven,
> And at each careless hammer-fall
>   A human heart is riven.
>
> And worse than all, the human slave,
>   The sport of lust, and pride, and scorn!
> Plucked off the crown his Maker gave,
>   His regal manhood gone!

"Mr. Pipes," she said.

"Yes, my dear," he replied, setting his book down.

"Why did freedom-loving Americans keep slaves as long as they did?"

Mr. Pipes gazed into the fire before answering.

Drew stopped pacing.

"I remember you telling us," said Drew, "about John Newton, the former slave captain; he helped end slavery in England."

"He did, indeed," replied Mr. Pipes. "Newton as a true Christian and follower of Christ's Law believed loving one's neighbor meant treating everyone with respect and justice—including slaves."

Dr. Dudley entered the room.

"If I may remind us all," he said. "We ended slavery in England long before—goodness knows—ever so long before you Americans got around to it."

"True enough. Slavery had been around a long time by Whittier's day," agreed Mr. Pipes. "Though many believed freeing the slaves was the right thing to do, nevertheless, Americans clung to slavery, for many reasons. Some wanted to preserve the original Constitutional rights of the states to regulate or abolish the institution of slavery on terms that would best ensure each state's economic and social stability. Others simply feared the social or political change that would come after freeing slaves."

"The changes came anyway," said Drew. "Boy, did they ever. We study a lot about the Civil War in school."

"But men like John Eliot and Samuel Davies loved slaves and taught them to read and took the gospel to them," said Annie, frowning.

"Oh, many Christians argued," said Mr. Pipes, "that African slaves were actually much better off under American slavery than ever they could have been in benighted Africa in the nineteenth century."

"Was that true?" asked Annie.

"True or not," replied Mr. Pipes, "one can never justify a slave system, African or American, that involves kidnapping and separating families. The fact that God brings good out of evil never justifies the evil."

"That makes sense," said Drew.

"One African girl, captured by other Africans and sold to a trader, was chained on board a slave ship and taken to America—she was only seven years old. About the time of Samuel Davies's death in 1761, the Wheatleys, a Christian family, purchased her at a Boston slave market. They named her Phillis and raised her as their own child, teaching

her to read the Bible and to love the Lord. She studied Latin, Greek, and English literature, and soon she began writing poetry of her own. At thirteen, her first poem appeared in print and she soon became a well-known poet with whom, I'm told, George Washington corresponded."

"It sounds to me like she was considerably better off here than there," said Dr. Dudley, from behind a two-day-old newspaper.

"But being a slave—some one's property," said Annie.

"Well, godly young Phillis," continued Mr. Pipes, "made the very most of her trials, and in one poem she actually expresses deep gratitude to the Lord for bringing her to America where she heard the gospel and became a Christian. It goes like this:

> 'Twas mercy brought me from my *Pagan* land,
> Taught my benighted soul to understand
> That there's a God, that there's a *Savior* too:
> Once I redemption neither sought nor knew.
>
> Some view our sable race with scornful eye,
> 'Their colour is a diabolical dye.'
> Remember, *Christians*, *Negroes*, black as Cain,
> May be refin'd, and join th'angelic train.

"What would have happened if she had never come," said Annie. "She would have never become a Christian—or a poet. But to be dragged here in such a cruel way...."

"Except that God obviously chose her," said Drew, sitting down on the hearth. "But making her a slave does seem kind of a funny way to make her a Christian. Then again, many slaves became Christians under Mr. Davies's preaching—probably lots of them."

"God's ways are high above ours, children," said Mr. Pipes. "Many New England slave holders treated their slaves kindly; Puritan Cotton Mather said, 'My servants are in some sense my children.' Nevertheless, it is a mystery of Providence that so many black slaves embraced Christianity instead of hating it as the white master's religion."

"I suppose in Phillis Wheatley's poem she was being 'content to fill a little space if [God] be glorified,'" said Annie, quoting from her favorite hymn.

"That was the right way for her to look at it," said Drew.

"Ah, yes," said Mr. Pipes. "But how ought slaveholders to have looked at slavery? In any case, Phillis Wheatley's life was considerably finer than life for many slaves laboring in some regions of America."

"What was life like for a slave in Mr. Whittier's day?" asked Annie.

"American slavery in Whittier's time too often divided children from their parents and wives from their husbands, and national laws protected abusive masters and forced sympathetic people to return runaway slaves. Although the cruel importation of slaves from Africa to America became illegal, some white slave owners effectively bred slaves for market, distributing them around the country to the highest bidder."

"That sounds awful," said Annie.

"If I may interject," interjected Dr. Dudley, "your brand of slavery sounds rather inconsistent with your high-sounding 'All men are created equal.' American liberty! Humph! I suspect many a slave scratched his woolly pate over that one."

He crossed his legs and resumed reading his newspaper.

"You will remember, my good doctor," replied Mr. Pipes, "that we, likewise, had slavery in England."

"Yes, but I," he looked down his long nose from around his newspaper, "never claimed to believe all that rot about liberty and equality."

"Yes, well," said Mr. Pipes, his eyebrows aloft. "Whittier and the Quakers led many other Americans in the worthy fight to free slaves—the Quaker Meeting House just down the road was a station in the Underground Railroad through which many slaves fleeing to Canada passed. Some abolitionists, however, went much further in their zeal and actually used terrorism and murder to achieve their goal. Meanwhile, as slave owners, politicians and abolitionists fought for their objectives, the majority of slaves continued faithfully serving their masters."

"Were very many of the slaves still Christians, by this time?" asked Drew.

"Yes," said Mr. Pipes, "some of them profoundly in love with our Lord in the midst of slavery. Many of the Christian slaves developed their own religious experience shaped by the difficulties and limited opportunities of their lives.

"You remember that Davies's slave converts loved singing day or night—especially the hymns of Isaac Watts. Well, in 1801, Richard Allen, founding bishop of the African Methodist Episcopal Church, published the first hymnal for use by an all-black congregation. It consisted mostly of Watts and Wesley but introduced the wandering refrain to their hymns. By Whittier's day, a kind of singing developed among black Christians called the *spiritual*. It grew out of improvisations of hymns and refrains and out of the work chants sung in the cotton fields from 'can't-see-mornin' to can't-see-night,' as the slaves called their day."

"That's a long day," said Annie.

"What did a spiritual sound like?" asked Drew.

"They generally followed a call-and-response pattern, with a leader singing out and, before he finished, the congregation overlapping his voice with theirs. Slaves sang their spirituals using flatted tones, a bending of the pitch that could help produce a soaring, or sometimes wailing, feeling in the singers. This kind of singing lent itself to considerable foot stomping, hand clapping, and generally swaying about."

"What did they sing about in spirituals?" asked Annie.

"Many of these spirituals understandably took long-suffering and a longing for the joys of heaven for their themes."

"Do you know any?" asked Drew.

"Well, perhaps the most universally known spiritual," said Mr. Pipes, "is 'Swing Low, Sweet Chariot.' Have you heard that one?"

"Sure," said Annie and Drew together.

"I think almost all Americans know it," said Annie.

And they sang from memory the chorus:

> Swing low, sweet chariot,
> Comin' for to carry me home,
> Swing low, sweet chariot,
> Comin' for to carry me home.

"Of course someone had to have thought up the original words and music for the spirituals," continued Mr. Pipes. "But for most of them we do not know the name of the humble saints who authored and composed the songs."

"Did Phillis Wheatley write any spirituals?" asked Annie.

"No, she would, no doubt, have sung the hymns of Isaac Watts," replied Mr. Pipes. "I do seem to recall another favorite well-known by 1865, sung in schools for black children in the south, and entitled, 'Nobody Knows de Trouble I've Had.'"

"That sounds a little familiar," said Annie.

Mr. Pipes hummed and clapped slowly with the simple melody. Soon, Annie and Drew joined in:

> Nobody knows de trouble I've had,
> Nobody knows but Jesus,
> Nobody knows de trouble I've had,
> Glory hallelu!

"This is the refrain," continued Mr. Pipes, "and would have been sung with the caller singing a line and the congregation responding with the next. Then folks would sing a verse, then the chorus again, over and over."

"But Mr. Pipes," said Annie, holding back a giggle, "Your British accent's all wrong for this kind of singing. You've got to—well, relax, loosen up a bit."

"Maybe a little twang in your voice would help," suggested Drew.

Dr. Dudley rolled his eyes.

"Yes, well, I will make whatever corrections in intonation of which I am capable," said Mr. Pipes, with a chuckle. "I am reminded that children often enjoy acting out some of the lines of this spiritual."

"How does that work?" asked Drew.

"Well now," said Mr. Pipes clearing his throat and rising to his feet in the middle of the room. He adjusted his necktie. "I will attempt to maintain some decorum and dignity whilst I demonstrate." He cleared his throat. Then, with swoops and dips in his voice he sang. Annie and Drew nearly burst at his painful efforts at singing with an American southern accent:

> Sometimes I'm up, sometimes I'm down,
> O yes, Lord!

He squatted part way, and smiling he continued:

> Sometimes I'm almost on de groun',
> O yes, Lord!

Squatting lower still, he began to teeter and wobble on his heels. Annie and Drew hopped to their feet, and laughing they took his arms and helped steady him. Then they joined in; clapping, singing, and squatting lower and lower through the verses over again.

> Sometimes I'm up, sometimes I'm down,
>   O yes, Lord!
> Sometimes I'm almost on de groun',
>   O yes, Lord!
>
> Nobody knows de trouble I've had,
>   Nobody knows but Jesus,
> Nobody knows de trouble I've had,
>   Glory hallelu!

Dr. Dudley peered out from behind his newspaper. Annie noticed his foot bobbing in time with the rhythm. They continued:

> What make ole Satan hate me so?
>   O yes, Lord!
> Because he got me once and he let me go!
>   O yes, Lord!

And then it happened. Dr. Dudley, lured by the lively strains, threw aside his paper and jumped to his feet, clapping his hands with the rhythm, and he joined in the chorus improvising a flatted tone bridge: "There ain't—"

> Nobody knows de trouble I've had,
>   Nobody knows but Jesus,
> Nobody knows de trouble I've had,
>   Glory hallelu!

"One more time, now," yelled Dr. Dudley. And he sang: "Oh yeah, there just ain't nobody who—"

Mr. Pipes waited until just the right moment and then came in with the children, overlapping Dr. Dudley's voice with:

> Nobody knows de trouble I've had,
>   Nobody knows but Jesus,
> Nobody knows de trouble I've had,
>   Glory hallelu!

❖ ❖ ❖

It took Dr. Dudley some time to recover himself after joining them so heartily in singing the spiritual. But after a fresh pot of tea and several slices of toast dripping in butter and smothered in marmalade he showed clear signs of recovery.

"I've prepared well, if I do say so myself," he said, smoothing his moustache with his thumb and index finger. He peered out the window at a gray bird pecking hungrily at the birdseed he'd set out earlier.

"I'm sure our feathered friend appreciates your foresight," said Mr. Pipes.

"Yes, yes," beamed Dr. Dudley. "*They* are most appreciative creatures."

Mr. Pipes sat before the fire humming a tune with his hymnal open on his lap.

Annie pulled her chair closer and listened.

Drew came back into the room after clomping around where the firewood was kept in the old summer kitchen. He lay a coil of Dr. Dudley's rope down by the hearth and listened.

"Sounds kind of like another spiritual," said Drew.

"It's a beautiful melody," said Annie. "It sounds kind of somber—almost melancholy." She hummed with Mr. Pipes.

"Is it a spiritual?" she asked.

"One might call 'Southern Harmony' a derivative of a spiritual," replied Mr. Pipes. "Certainly influenced by slave singing in the mid-nineteenth century."

"It doesn't sound as—well, as bouncy," said Annie.

"No, no this is definitely not a foot stomper," smiled Mr. Pipes, humming the first few bars again. "'Southern Harmony' might best be called a regional folk hymn in the strophic form—you'll learn about that, Drew, as you keep up on those music lessons."

"I think it sounds dignified," said Drew, humming. "I like it."

"But it sounds—what's the word?" said Annie, "passionate, too?"

"It is ode-like," agreed Mr. Pipes, "a melody well-suited to the lofty emotion evoked by the words celebrating our Lord's wondrous love for sinners."

"Can we sing it?" asked Annie.

Mr. Pipes, his voice so suited to lofty, passionate expressions of devotion, led them:

> What wondrous love is this, O my soul, O my soul,
> What wondrous love is this, O my soul,
> What wondrous love is this that caused the Lord of bliss
> To bear the dreadful curse for my soul, for my soul,
> To bear the dreadful curse for my soul!
>
> To God and to the Lamb, I will sing, I will sing,
> To God and to the Lamb, I will sing;
> To God and to the Lamb, who is the great I AM,
> While millions join the theme, I will sing, I will sing,
> While millions join the theme, I will sing!
>
> And when from death I'm free, I'll sing on, I'll sing on,
> And when from death I'm free, I'll sing on;
> And when from death I'm free, I'll sing and joyful be,
> And through eternity I'll sing on, I'll sing on,
> And through eternity I'll sing on!

"The tune ends without completely ending," said Drew, when they finished.

"Maybe that's because," said Annie, reading the last lines again, "because when we sing it we're suppose to realize that words cannot fully express the answer to the question, 'What wondrous love is this?'"

"So the music helps us continue thinking—" Drew broke off, "—what's the other word?"

"Meditating?" offered Mr. Pipes.

"Yeah, *meditating* about it all," continued Drew, "even after we finish singing."

"Precisely."

What Wondrous Love Is This

How great is the love the Father has lavished on us, that we should be called
children of God! 1 John 3:1

1. What won-drous love is this, O my soul, O my soul, what
won-drous love is this, O my soul! What won-drous love is
this that caused the Lord of bliss to bear the dread-ful curse for my
soul, for my soul, to bear the dread-ful curse for my soul!

2. To God and to the Lamb, I will sing, I will sing, to
God and to the Lamb, I will sing; to God and to the
Lamb, who is the great I AM, while mil-lions join the theme, I will
sing, I will sing, while mil-lions join the theme, I will sing!

3. And when from death I'm free, I'll sing on, I'll sing on, and
when from death I'm free, I'll sing on; and when from death I'm
free, I'll sing and joy-ful be, and through e-ter-ni-ty I'll sing
on, I'll sing on, and through e-ter-ni-ty I'll sing on!

American folk hymn

WONDROUS LOVE 12.9.12.9.
The Southern Harmony, 1835

Chapter Nine

Ray Palmer
1808–1887

Be this my joy, that evermore
Thou rulest all things at Thy will;
Thy sovereign wisdom I adore,
And calmly, sweetly, trust Thee still.

"I think it's stopped snowing," said Drew, later that afternoon. "When can we go outside?"

"Snow's piled everywhere," said Annie. "I doubt we can even get the door open—and it still looks awfully cold out there." She shivered.

"Well, we shall someday be able to get out," said Dr. Dudley, setting a pair of skis over a crate filled with firewood. "I'll just tune and wax these skis so we are ready the moment we become un-snowbound."

"And then we'll leave for Boston," said Annie, "and home?"

Drew frowned.

"There will be, I should think," replied Mr. Pipes, "a digging-out period, during which time roads and airports will need to work very hard to reopen. Perhaps a couple of days beyond the big snowfall, perhaps more."

"I'd go for more," said Drew grinning.

Annie groaned inwardly. Oh, she loved it here with Mr. Pipes; what could be better? But Christmas with her parents and Mr. Pipes—she had to get him there somehow.

Drew watched as Dr. Dudley sighted down the curved underside of the skis and then ran a file over the metal edges with care.

"Can I help?" asked Drew.

"This one's ready," said Dr. Dudley. "Now rub a thin layer of wax on the tip and tail."

He took a stick of wax softening on the hearth and handed it to Drew. Drew thought it looked like a giant color crayon without any paper around it. He sniffed the warm wax; it smelled like a rough-hewn chalet in the mountains; like hot tea after a day of skiing through pine forests on powdery slopes. He felt a wave of excitement come over him. He'd never skied before—not much opportunity in a place where it was seventy-five degrees at Christmas time. But here he was—about to learn. He looked out the window at the drifted snow covering everything; now, if there was just some way to go fishing.

"—No, no, Drew. Pay attention. No wax on the curved bit in the middle," said Dr. Dudley, "just tips and tails. You'll need that rough bit for the gripping."

Opening and closing her sketchbook, Annie sat next to Mr. Pipes at the fire, and watched.

"How long do you think we'll be snowbound?" asked Annie.

"I really do not know, my dear," said Mr. Pipes. "But the snow has stopped—that is a good sign."

"Yeah, stopped for now," said Drew. "The caretaker said winter snowstorms can last for ages," he went on, feeling better about being snowbound if he could learn to ski.

"What if we get stuck here," said Annie, "and can't get home for Christmas—or even for school?"

"I must gently remind you, my dear," said Mr. Pipes. "That all of this is outside our control. God makes snowstorms, so let us simply enjoy His Providence. We shall trust Him to work out the schedule.

"Oh, snow is so very lovely," he added looking out the frosty window.

Annie knew Mr. Pipes was right. She felt somewhat better and opened her sketchbook to her poem.

"I like the idea about no school, though," said Drew, running the wax along the bottom of another ski. "What did school kids do in Whittier's day when it snowed—broke their hearts, I bet?"

"Well, in rural New England," said Mr. Pipes. "Many children learned at home."

"I think I'd like that," said Annie.

Drew sobered. "Only problem is that when you got snowed in—you'd still have school."

"Problem?" said Mr. Pipes, raising his eyebrows and smiling.

"Not far away in Rhode Island," he continued, "in 1808, only the year after Mr. Whittier was born, your American hymn writer, Ray Palmer came into the world; his long life would, like Whittier's, span much of the century."

"Did he go to school at home?" asked Annie.

"He did," replied Mr. Pipes.

"No snow days for him," said Drew.

"I suppose not," said Mr. Pipes. "As a young man, Ray Palmer worked as a clerk in Boston. One day he heard the gospel preached at Park Street Church on what they called 'Brimstone Corner,' because of the fervent gospel preaching from that pulpit. God's grace so flooded his soul that he longed to proclaim the gospel as a minister. After earning his degree at Yale in 1830, he taught school whilst studying theology. He was eventually ordained as a Congregationalist minister in 1835 and served the Lord tirelessly for many years."

"When did he write his first real hymn?" asked Annie.

"The best of his thirty-eight hymns he wrote in his youth, soon after graduating from Yale. His well-known hymn, 'My Faith Looks Up to Thee,' he wrote in a little notebook kept handy in his pocket. It became so well-known that many American Christians, eager for a sensational story and certain that it must have been written out of some dramatic experience, begged him to tell them how he wrote it."

"Like on the deck of a warship," said Drew.

"Or whilst snowbound," suggested Dr. Dudley, who they never were quite sure was listening.

"Didn't I hear somewhere," he went on, "that Augustus Toplady wrote 'Rock of Ages' on the back of a playing card and it is housed in some American library—but no one seems to know which library."

"I fear," said Mr. Pipes, "there was a time when it may have been found in more than one library."

"How could that be?" asked Annie.

"Pure fabrication, satisfying an appetite for sensation," said Dr. Dudley, shortly. "Reminds me of medieval bishops claiming to have a piece of the cross housed in their cathedral—one might have reconstructed Noah's Ark, so great was the quantity of sacred kindling!"

"No kidding!" said Drew.

"Well, what *was* Mr. Palmer's story?" asked Annie.

"He told all," went on Mr. Pipes. "He wrote it out of 'no external occasion whatever.'"

Annie smiled.

"He wrote it, perhaps," speculated Mr. Pipes, "finding inspiration from Hebrews 12:1, 2—'Let us run with patience the race that is set before us, looking unto Jesus the Author and Perfecter of our faith....'"

Mr. Pipes recited portions of the hymn:

> My faith looks up to Thee,
> Thou Lamb of Calvary,
> Savior Divine ...
> As Thou hast died for me,
> O may my love to Thee,
> Pure, warm, and changeless be,
> A living fire! ...

"Young Mr. Palmer tucked the poem away," continued Mr. Pipes, "until on a street in Boston, a year or more later, he met the musician Lowell Mason, who asked him to contribute a hymn for a book he was publishing. Mason trained the children's choir at Park Street Church, Boston, where the Lord first opened Palmer's spiritual eyes and saved him. Mason wrote many tunes that have remained the settings for American and English hymns. Some are very good, indeed, though some sound as if they might be better suited for singing around a campfire on the prairie.

"About the same time, Mason also asked the Baptist pastor Samuel Francis Smith to contribute a hymn for his book. Smith came across a lovely patriotic melody and was inspired to write 'My Country 'Tis of Thee.' He was so carried away with patriotic fervor, he wrote it all in only half an hour. Little did he know, the tune that inspired him was already the tune for England's national anthem, 'God Save the Queen!'"

"You don't say!" said Dr. Dudley. "That is a story to remember."

"Mason's children's choir sang 'My Country 'Tis of Thee,' to a different tune, for the first time on July 4, 1832. Frankly, it is not truly great poetry, and it is not a hymn to God as much as a hymn to America—a growing problem, I fear. One president of Harvard said of the anthem, 'Did ever a piece of doggerel win a man such fame!'"

"So, did Mr. Palmer show Mr. Mason his hymn?" asked Annie.

"Yes, and after Mason read it, he exclaimed, 'Mr. Palmer, you may live many years and do a good many things, but I think you will be best known to posterity as the author of "My Faith Looks Up to Thee."'"

"Is it his best?" asked Drew.

"That is hard to say, for he wrote at least two others equally excellent. Another hymn of faith about seeing the unseen is particularly fine. Let me find it in my hymnal so you can follow along."

Annie leaned on the old man's shoulder and drank in the poetry while he read:

> Jesus, these eyes have never seen
> That radiant form of Thine;
> The veil of sense hangs dark between
> Thy blessed face and mine.
>
> I see Thee not, I hear Thee not,
> Yet art Thou oft with me;
> And earth hath ne'er so dear a spot
> As where I meet with Thee.

Yet though I have not seen, and still
Must rest in faith alone;
I love Thee, dearest Lord, and will,
Unseen, but not unknown.

When death these mortal eyes shall seal,
And still this throbbing heart,
The rending veil shall Thee reveal,
All glorious as Thou art.

When he finished reading, the only sound was the pensive humming of the fire.

"Didn't Whittier's hymn," asked Annie, at last, "have something in it about leading us from ourselves to God?"

"It did," said Mr. Pipes.

"Well, I think that hymn helps lead us from ourselves to God," said Annie wistfully.

"I would agree," said Mr. Pipes with a sigh. "But too often Christian singing in worship, even by sincere people, entertains and amuses but does little to lead us away from ourselves to God. Alas, music designed to entertain accomplishes quite the reverse."

Drew rubbed the wax slowly over another ski.

"It is a problem seeing the Lord—really seeing Him," he said, "when all the earthly stuff you can actually see—with your real eyes."

"'The veil of sense,'" quoted Annie, "'hangs dark between.'"

"Yeah," said Drew. "So it must have been a problem for Mr. Palmer, too."

"But 'death these mortal eyes shall seal,'" said Mr. Pipes. "And then what?"

Dr. Dudley's file scraped rhythmically.

"I guess that's what makes it such a perfect hymn," continued Drew thoughtfully. "Mr. Palmer helps us see what we can't see, but what will still be there when we die and our eyes can't see anymore."

"That gives something of the lie," said Dr. Dudley quietly, "to the old adage: 'Seeing is believing.'"

"Faith, of course," said Mr. Pipes, "is believing without seeing. Faith is the substance of things hoped for, the certain and objective knowledge of things not yet seen. And only God's Spirit can give us that."

❖ ❖ ❖

"Did anyone else hear it?" asked Dr. Dudley, later, as the whiteness outside deepened into the gray evening.

"Hear what?" asked Drew.

"Scratching. I am almost certain I heard scratching."

"Do you think it's some animal caught out in the storm?" asked Annie.

"Well if it is," said Dr. Dudley, "I really do not see how it could have survived this cold. And there's nothing to eat with all this snow piled everywhere. Let us be silent and listen for it again."

They sat stiffly listening. Wind still blew against the windows, and though no snow fell from the gray sky, gusts of powdery snow swirled against the windows from time to time. Annie couldn't hear anything that sounded like an animal scratching.

"Maybe I imagined it," sighed Dr. Dudley, at last.

"Let us hope you did," said Mr. Pipes.

❖ ❖ ❖

Dinner was a sumptuous affair that evening. Dr. Dudley made a heaping chicken pot pie, complaining all the while that he had made untiring efforts in Boston to secure kidneys and tinned steak for an English—and much superior pie—but to no avail.

"This will simply have to do," he said, looking proudly at the golden crust as he set it on the table.

"Oh, I'm sure this'll be even better," said Annie, gratefully.

"Oh, I believe our soup is ready on the stove," he said. "Annie do ladle it into bowls for us. And Drew, you slice bread. Mr.

Pipes, I fear I could get you no Stilton or Cheshire; this ghastly orange cheese must serve in their place."

"You have simply outdone yourself, my good man,' said Mr. Pipes.

"Oh, just you wait, Mr. Pipes," said Dr. Dudley. "I have some wonderful things planned for Christmas dinner."

Annie looked up quickly at Mr. Pipes. He smiled in return.

After the blessing, Drew bit into an enormous bite of pie.

"Umm, ooh, [munch, munch] ah," he groaned in ecstasy, his eyes showing white as he chewed. "This is [munch, swallow] too good!"

"What's that flavor?" asked Annie, after she'd finished her first and much smaller bite than Drew's.

"I've seasoned all with thyme," beamed Dr. Dudley.

"The best seasoning of all!" said Annie, nodding her head and turning to Mr. Pipes.

"You are entirely too kind," smiled Mr. Pipes, tipping his white head at her.

"I get it!" said Drew. "Thyme the spice, and time—well, time like on the calendar."

"And lots of it, as seen in white hair and aging joints," said Mr. Pipes, laughing.

"No, I was thinking of time in another way,' said Annie more soberly. She smiled at Mr. Pipes. "Time as in—wisdom."

"Here's to wisdom," agreed Drew, taking another enormous bite of pie.

◈ ◈ ◈

"You said Mr. Palmer wrote another best hymn," said Annie, as they sat comfortably around the fire in the Garden Room after dinner.

"Pass the shortbread, please," said Drew. "I love it when they dribble these lines of chocolate on 'em," he added, biting into a cookie.

"I did, indeed," said Mr. Pipes, smiling, candlelight flickering warmly and casting shadows upwards from his shiny cheeks.

"Mr. Palmer represents the last major American hymn writer—and some would argue the greatest—who wrote his hymns from a Calvinistic understanding of God's Word."

"Like Mr. Davies and Mr. Dwight," said Drew.

"And like so many of our British hymn writers," added Dr. Dudley.

"You never cease to amaze me," said Mr. Pipes.

"Thank you," said Dr. Dudley, raising his chin several degrees.

"I frankly can never tell if you are listening," said Mr. Pipes.

"But I am," replied Dr. Dudley, almost smugly.

"How does Mr. Palmer's next best hymn go?" asked Annie, thumbing through Mr. Pipes' hymnal.

"Perhaps, not quite so poetically fine as 'Jesus These Eyes Have Never Seen,'" said Mr. Pipes, "Mr. Palmer's, 'Lord My Weak Thought in Vain Would Climb,' nevertheless, is a marvelous hymn exploring the unsearchable ways of predestination and God's all-wise rule of all His creatures and all their actions. In it he acknowledges how weak and inadequate we are.…"

Mr. Pipes spread his arms and looked upward as he recited:

> To search Thy great eternal plan,
> Thy sovereign counsels, born of love
> Long ages ere the world began.

"He puts in poetry the questions and objections we—with clenched teeth—pose to the Almighty:

> When my dim reason would demand
> Why that, or this, Thou dost ordain,
> By some vast deep I seem to stand,
> Whose secrets I must ask in vain.

"Then he takes us poetically by the hand and shows us how we ought to respond in faith to doctrines we don't like:

> When doubts disturb my troubled breast,
> And all is dark as night to me,

Here, as on solid rock, I rest,—
That so it seemeth good to Thee.

"Then, and only then," continued Mr. Pipes, "will we come—and not just begrudgingly—admitting that God is sovereign, all the while wishing it were not so. No, no, Christians only find sweet joy when we embrace and *adore* what we formerly questioned and even hated about God's decrees:

Be this my joy, that evermore
Thou rulest all things at Thy will;
Thy sovereign wisdom I adore,
And calmly, sweetly, trust Thee still.

❈ ❈ ❈

Just before crawling into bed, Annie scraped a hole in the frosty windowpane in her room and peered out. She watched the clouds thinning and moonlight peeking through and glowing on the drifted whiteness all around. She shivered and hopped into bed, and with the candle flame quivering on the walls, she lay listening to the muffled stillness of the night. So, the storm was over, but there was still that digging out time—which could be really fun. She needed to trust God more, like in Mr. Palmer's hymn—after all, He sent this snowstorm in the first place.

She opened her sketchbook and reread her first verse. Then after reading Psalm 86 again she began writing. Mr. Palmer needed no 'external occasion whatever,' she thought, crunching her teeth into the orange paint and soft wood of her pencil. After writing, scratching out, erasing and writing again, she scrunched her knees up under her chin and read:

In you, O Lord, I put my trust;
Salvation is from you.
From dawn to dusk I call your name;
Your mercy's ever new.

Hmm, maybe she'd show it to Mr. Pipes tomorrow—maybe.

My Faith Looks Up to Thee

*Let us run with perseverance the race marked out for us. Let us fix our eyes on Jesus,
the author and perfecter of our faith. Heb. 12:1, 2*

1. My faith looks up to thee, thou Lamb of Cal - va - ry,
2. May thy rich grace im- part strength to my faint - ing heart,
3. While life's dark maze I tread, and griefs a - round me spread,
4. When ends life's tran - sient dream, when death's cold, sul - len stream

Sav - ior di - vine: now hear me while I pray, take all my
my zeal in - spire; as thou hast died for me, O may my
be thou my guide; bid dark - ness turn to day, wipe sor - row's
shall o'er me roll, blest Sav - ior, then, in love, fear and dis -

guilt a - way, O let me from this day be whol - ly thine.
love to thee, pure, warm, and change - less be, a liv - ing fire.
tears a - way, nor let me ev - er stray from thee a - side.
trust re- move; O bear me safe a - bove, a ran - somed soul.

Ray Palmer, 1830

OLIVET 6.6.4.6.6.6.4.
Lowell Mason, 1832

Chapter Ten

Matthias Loy
1863

The law of God is good and wise
And sets His will before our eyes,
Shows us the way of righteousness,
And dooms to death when we transgress.

Christmas Eve dawned cold and clear, with no wind; though snow lay piled everywhere, the storm was over. Drew fidgeted through breakfast, gazing fixedly at the brightness out the window. Dr. Dudley and Mr. Pipes discussed over cups of tea the wisdom of making a foray out of doors. Annie smiled in wonder as the sunlight sparkled brilliantly on the snow.

"I'd love to go outside," she said, hesitantly, "but it looks so perfect—I'd hate to mess it up with footprints."

"How about *ski* prints!" said Drew.

"*Tracks*, ski *tracks*, Drew," corrected Dr. Dudley.

❖ ❖ ❖

"Hey, what's the deal?" asked Drew, moments later as they bundled up. "I noticed this yesterday—there's only three pairs of skis?"

Mr. Pipes smiled and turned silently to Dr. Dudley.

"Naturally," replied Dr. Dudley, defensively. "You didn't actually think I would facilitate putting Mr. Pipes in harm's way skiing?"

"But it won't be as fun without him," said Drew.

Annie gripped Drew's arm hard and scowled at him, tilting her head toward Dr. Dudley.

"But he will be safe when we are finished," replied Dr. Dudley. "My dear man, bones grow brittle at your age—one must be careful. Skiing is for the young and hale," he concluded, zipping up his parka and patting his chest.

"So Mr. Pipes has to stay inside?" asked Annie, looping her arm in his.

"Wait a minute," interrupted Drew. "I found a bunch of stuff in the summer kitchen yesterday: a big old sled and a pair of snowshoes."

"Snowshoes are much slower," mused Dr. Dudley, "more safe."

"We shall never get the door open from inside with snow drifted so high," said Mr. Pipes. "How about if we exit through a window?"

"And this one," said Drew, "has snow right up to the sill."

Dr. Dudley and Drew pried it open and passed skis and snowshoes out onto the powdery drift.

"I shall choose a slower more meandering pace," said Mr. Pipes, smiling and strapping the snowshoes to his feet.

"Yes, yes, as you should," said Dr. Dudley. "Now, children, I shall teach you how to ski as I learned when a child on winter holiday in Wales."

He helped them into the ski bindings, showed them how to put their hand up through the strap on the ski poles and grip pole and strap for better pushing on each stride. Then he demonstrated swinging arms and poles forward as he brought one ski then the other into the clean white snow.

His jaw set, Drew plunged forward staggering at first, his weight shifting awkwardly from ski to ski. Dr. Dudley's skis left a tidy evenly spaced track behind him. Drew decided he'd try passing him.

Annie felt excited and a little nervous as she took her first tentative strides. She frowned at Drew's mangled, crisscrossed track messing up the snow next to Dr. Dudley's. She knew which one to follow. The powder-like snow creaked under her skis. She breathed in the cold winter air scented with fir trees and a hint of smoke from their fire.

Mr. Pipes followed behind, breathing deeply and smiling at the frosty whiteness surrounding them.

"Lovely, isn't it, my dear," he said to Annie, as they brought up the rear together.

Annie stopped and gazed around. "Oh, it is. Everything looks so different—so pure and clean. I love it."

"'Wash me and I shall be whiter than snow,'" said Mr. Pipes. "So says Holy Scripture. Ah, and a wonderful metaphor, indeed."

"Sounds like poetry," said Annie, watching the graceful curve of her ski tips as she slid forward and they parted the snow.

"It is the finest poetry," said Mr. Pipes. "From Psalm 51, David's humble penitence after violating the precious Law of God."

Annie frowned.

Mr. Pipes went on: "I read just this morning from Psalm 19 about the unsurpassed splendor of God's Law. 'The law of the Lord is perfect,' says David, 'trustworthy, right, radiant, pure, precious, and sweet.'"

Mr. Pipes paused in the snow, saying the adjectives with emphasis, his gloved hand gesturing with each word.

"But isn't grace more precious than law," said Annie. "I mean, we're saved by grace, not by keeping the law, right?"

"True, but my dear, we are saved by grace from the *punishment* of our *violation* of God's law—not from the law itself. We were redeemed to obey, not to continue in sin; and it is God's law we must obey."

Again Annie stopped. "You know, Mr. Pipes, we go to a worship center back home with the Smiths, and I remember a song we sometimes sing; something like, 'Free From the Law, O Happy Condition....' That doesn't exactly sound like the Psalms."

"No, I fear it does not," said Mr. Pipes. "But we shall talk more of this later. Just now, Drew and Dr. Dudley have found a hill, and there goes Dr. Dudley—do be careful, dear man," he called.

"Nothing to fear," came Dr. Dudley's voice confidently, as he bent his knees and swished down the hill.

With a "Yahoo!" Drew followed.

"Come try it Annie," called Dr. Dudley.

"Yeah, it's great," said Drew, looking like a frosted Christmas tree as he picked himself up out of the snow. "Stopping's a little dicey, though."

"I'll watch for a bit," she called back, laughing. "You didn't break anything, I hope?"

"No way; it's all soft snow," he said, slogging up the hill. "You've gotta try it."

"Well, maybe."

Several minutes later Annie felt the crisp air rushing against her red cheeks and swishing in her ears. From under her wool hat, her long hair streamed behind as she skied down the slope.

"Bend your knees, my dear," called Dr. Dudley. "Weight on the downhill ski. That's better."

❖ ❖ ❖

Annie warmed her hands around a steaming mug of hot chocolate. The Garden Room smelled like wet wool and steam drifted from soaked mittens, hats and socks drying on the screen before the fire.

Drew put on a fresh log.

"I should have closed the window," said Dr. Dudley, blowing on his hands.

"However, that might have made our getting back into the house," said Mr. Pipes, "a trifle difficult. You did the right thing; house needed a good airing and we'll be warm in a few minutes."

"This hot chocolate is so good," said Annie, sipping the hot liquid.

Drew drained his mug and looked up with an expression on his face Annie had seen many times before.

"Dr. Dudley," said Drew, eyeing him, "which is better, American chocolate or British?"

"It is not even a close call, my boy," said Dr. Dudley, dismissing Drew's question with a wave of his hand. "*English* chocolate is the very finest."

"Did you bring any with you from England?" asked Drew.

"Of course," said Dr. Dudley. "It is difficult to get British-made chocolate in the *colonies*; I did purchase some of yours in Boston, you understand, as a last resort. One never wants to run out of chocolate—even inferior chocolate."

Annie whispered in Mr. Pipes' ear, "I know what Drew's up to."

"As do I, my dear, as do I," replied Mr. Pipes, winking at her.

"Chocolate, chocolate," said Drew, shaking his head. "English chocolate can't really be any better."

"The gauntlet has been delivered," said Dr. Dudley, slapping his fist in his palm. "We shall settle this trifling skirmish here and now."

He marched into the kitchen, mumbling something about keeping colonials in their proper place, and returned with two large packages of chocolate—one bold blue and the other chocolate brown. Drew licked his lips and grinned broadly at Annie and Mr. Pipes.

"Now then," said Dr. Dudley, pulling up a sideboard table and breaking each bar into squares. "Here are the rules of engagement: Americans on one side of the table, we British on the other. To neutralize the palate, a plain saltine wafer must be consumed between each sampling, thus—" Slitting his eyes at them from across the table, he munched viciously into a cracker.

Drew rubbed his hands together.

"Sometimes in the course of war," continued Dr. Dudley, "one must engage the enemy without mercy; we shall grant quarter to no one!"

"Take no prisoners!" cried Drew, grabbing a handful of chocolate squares and jumping into the fray.

For a moment the only sound was munching.

"Way too early to tell," said Drew, swallowing.

Mr. Pipes and Annie laughed and sampled the two chocolate bars.

"No fraternizing with the enemy, Pipes," said Dr. Dudley.

"Tolerable," said Drew, munching on two pieces of blue-labeled chocolate and reaching for another.

"Wait your turn, Drew," said Dr. Dudley. "We must fire in turn like gentlemen. This is no skulking war."

"Whatever you say," said Drew. "I could really get the hang of this if I just had more practice."

※ ※ ※

After clearing the field and Dr. Dudley triumphantly pronouncing, "The day is ours!" they digested their chocolate quietly around the fire, reading from the ample selection of books lining the walls of Mr. Whittier's house.

Annie closed Whittier's book of anti-slavery poetry after a while and looked critically at the poem she was writing in her sketchbook.

"Is it ready?" asked Mr. Pipes, looking at her over his glasses.

"Not quite yet," sighed Annie. "But I'll show it to you soon— I promise."

"Mr. Pipes," she said after a moment.

"Yes, my dear."

"Well, I've been thinking, and I'm not sure I quite understand what you were saying about God's law."

"Many stumble here, my dear," said Mr. Pipes. "Your American desire for freedom became for many simply a means of throwing off God's law in favor of self-government—that is, ruling their world by themselves and for themselves."

"Is that what's wrong with the song, 'Free From the Law, O Happy Condition'?"

"It just might be part of the problem," replied Mr. Pipes. "But that song, and many like it, represent a departure from theological hymns, like Ray Palmer's, in favor of gospel songs devoid of much doctrine, designed more to attract people to evangelistic camp meetings.

"As the teaching and admonishing function of hymns diminished, publishers of American hymnals chopped up the poetic lines and inserted them out of order in the musical score. Gone from the pages of the hymnal are the clear lines and verses of the poetry—wherein, formerly, the progression of thought, the parallels, and poetic conventions were so much more easily seen. Alas, in nineteenth-century singing, Americans thought it more important that the words appear under the notes than that they see the meaning of the poetry clearly. In this way, they forced the objective content of the words to take second place to the sound of the catchy tunes. This is still seen today in the way Americans print their hymnals.

"These new priorities emerging in American singing took their toll on objective content, making singing part of an evangelistic strategy for getting people saved. This produced, to be sure, many professions of faith but, I fear, very little spiritual change of heart.

"Themes like God's law and His sovereignty might offend an unbeliever, so those themes, although featured so much in the Psalms, are hardly seen at all in the gospel song singing after Palmer—a great loss, indeed."

"I do not wonder at any of this," sniffed Dr. Dudley, "democracies rarely produce other worldly things like great poetry expressive of high religious understanding and feeling because transcendence is so swallowed up by the here and now. You Americans are so infernally concerned about temporal liberties, money, and reforming society with laws and such things. *Our* historian Thomas Carlyle got it right when he declared American democracy 'all sail and no anchor.'"

"True," admitted Mr. Pipes. "But I must remind you, my good doctor, that America is actually a Constitutional republic, which includes some elements of democracy. Moreover, Britain today—make no mistake about it—is also a type of democratic republic."

"Pity," said Dr. Dudley, returning to his newspaper with a snap.

"So it was pretty much downhill after Mr. Palmer," said Drew, adjusting a log with a poker, sparks hissing upward.

"I am afraid so, my dears," said Mr. Pipes. "However, there were a few exceptions. One very fine hymn—one might call it the theological opposite, Annie, of your aforementioned gospel song—was published in 1863 by the German Lutheran immigrant to American, Matthias Loy. A gifted educator—president of Capital University in Columbus, Ohio, he wrote and translated a number of hymns for the Evangelical Lutheran Synod of Ohio. His very best hymn is a theologically rigorous exploration of the law of God based on Psalm 19. Master the truth expressed in these weighty lines and you will have a solid understanding of the role of God's law in the life of the Christian."

Mr. Pipes turned to the hymn in his hymnal and Drew looked at the name on the right side of the page.

"'Geistliche Lieder,' Wittenberg, 1543," read Drew, stumbling over the German. "Hey, this tune's from Luther's lifetime!"

"And Wittenberg's where Luther nailed his Ninety-five Theses on the church door," said Annie.

"So Mr. Loy used a three-hundred-year-old tune for his words," said Drew. "Might even be one of Luther's."

"A common practice," said Mr. Pipes. "Select an existing tune—a really grand one—then write your poetry in the same meter, using the same number of syllables."

Annie looked at Mr. Pipes. So if she made sure her poetry matched a common meter, she might have several tunes to sing it with.

Mr. Pipes hummed the tune and Annie and Drew quickly joined in the sober German melody.

"Now, let us add the words," said Mr. Pipes.

> The law of God is good and wise
> And sets His will before our eyes,
> Shows us the way of righteousness,
> And dooms to death when we transgress.
>
> Its light of holiness imparts
> The knowledge of our sinful hearts
> That we may see our lost estate
> And seek deliv'rance ere too late.
>
> To those who help in Christ have found

And would in works of love abound
It shows what deeds are His delight
And should be done as good and right.

When men the offered help disdain
And willfully in sin remain,
Its terror in their ear resounds
And keeps their wickedness in bounds.

The law is good; but since the fall
Its holiness condemns us all;
It dooms us for our sin to die
And has no power to justify.

To Jesus we for refuge flee,
Who from the curse has set us free,
And humbly worship at His throne,
Saved by His grace through faith alone.

When they finished, Annie was the first to speak.

"I feel like I'm back in Germany," she said.

"He did employ a compressed poetic style," said Mr. Pipes, "more typical of the German Reformation than of nineteenth-century American poetry."

"There's a lot there to think about," said Drew. "That last line reminds me of Luther's message of justification by faith alone."

"Mr. Loy's hymn sounds more like the Psalms," said Annie. "The law of God is good, but we can't keep it so it can't justify us—only God's grace does that. Oh, I think I need to study this one over and over."

"You'll find deeper truths to contemplate, here," said Mr. Pipes, "than you will in the song, 'Free From the Law, O Happy Condition,' much deeper, indeed. Master the scriptural argument in Loy's hymn and you will have a more biblical understanding of the role of the law than many ministers who should know better."

Annie and Drew read silently through the weighty words again.

◈ ◈ ◈

Dr. Dudley suddenly looked up from his book and cocked his ear.

"Did you hear it?" he hissed.

"Hear what?" whispered Annie.

He held up his hand for silence.

"Scratching," he whispered, pointing toward the kitchen.

"Yeah," said Drew. "I heard it a while ago."

"Shh!"

Dr. Dudley rose slowly and tip-toed to the kitchen door; the others followed.

"I don't see anything," said Drew, eyeing through the partially opened door.

"Wait!" said Annie, gripping his arm.

They all saw it at once. A black-haired creature with a distinct white stripe down its back and tail waddled merrily across the table, sniffing from side to side.

"Oh, dash it all!" said Dr. Dudley. "It's a skunk!"

"He's so cute!" squealed Annie in a whisper. "And he must have gotten terribly hungry during the storm."

"You will revise your opinion of him," hissed Dr. Dudley, "if he lifts that tail and sprays our food stores—the house and we will reek 'til doomsday. I thought skunks hibernated in winter; whatever is he doing up and about?"

"They are largely dormant in winter," whispered Mr. Pipes, "Though I am not sure they properly hibernate."

"I'll bet the warm winter followed by the big storm got the poor thing confused," said Drew.

"I see no possible way we can remove him to the outdoors without his spraying," said Mr. Pipes.

"Oh, and he's so hungry," said Annie. "He'd starve out in the snow."

"We must act fast," said Dr. Dudley. "Drew, grab a tin of corned beef from the boxes stored in the woodshed—but make no noise! Annie, get my leather bag, quickly!"

They watched as Dr. Dudley added several drops of liquid from one of the little bottles in his doctor's bag to the corned beef and stirred it up.

"You wouldn't!" said Annie.

"No I wouldn't," said Dr. Dudley. "It is not poison; merely an anesthetic—put the little fellow to sleep for a bit."

"Then what?" asked Drew.

Dr. Dudley checked the instruments in his bag.

"Surgery," he replied.

Annie looked at the razor-sharp scalpel and groaned.

"Now, pray I don't frighten the poor creature," he said as he slowly opened the door and set the saucer of corned beef on the floor.

"Surgery just because the poor thing's hungry?" hissed Annie in Dr. Dudley's ear, after he rejoined them. "What will you do next time *I'm* hungry?"

Dr. Dudley held his finger to his lips. They watched as the skunk lifted his nose in the air, his head bobbing until he turned and found the source of the scent. Its tail flicked—Dr. Dudley caught his breath. Then it turned and ambled toward the saucer of food.

"Come on, come on, fella," coaxed Dr. Dudley in a whisper. "Big bites—it's all yours."

The skunk sniffed at the corned beef.

"Now, fall to," urged Dr. Dudley.

After a cautious sampling, the skunk ravenously inhaled the mound of canned meat.

"How long will it take?" asked Drew, in a whisper.

As if to answer Drew's question, the furry creature curled up and with a contented sigh fell fast asleep.

Dr. Dudley burst into the room and whisked the skunk up onto the table. He scrubbed his hands and arms in the sink.

"Get me plenty of towels," he ordered. "Scrub your hands and prepare to assist me in the operating room."

"What are you going to do?" asked Annie, stroking the black and white fur of the sleeping animal.

"Remove the odor sac from near the anal glands," said Dr. Dudley.

"Isn't there some other way?" asked Annie, near tears.

"None," he replied shortly.

"But you're a *people* doctor," said Annie. "Have you ever done it before?"

"Never. But I have read something or other on the procedure."

"A dream fulfilled," said Mr. Pipes, smiling at his friend. "He always wanted to be a veterinary surgeon."

Dr. Dudley turned the skunk over and administered a more potent shot of anesthetic with a hypodermic needle.

"It's okay, little fella," said Annie, patting a paw comfortingly. "Oh, please, be careful," she added to Dr. Dudley.

"I intend to," he replied curtly. "Now, then, who will be my surgical assistant?"

Drew stared hard from the scalpel poised over the little skunk's undersides to the pan and sponge standing ready. He swallowed. Mr. Pipes put his arm on Drew's shoulder.

"Drew, perhaps you and I ought to see what we can do to make up a comfortable bed in which our patient might recover *after* surgery," said Mr. Pipes, leading him from the kitchen.

"I-I'll be your nurse," said Annie. "Just tell me what to do."

"Fetch Mr. Pipes's razor; we shall need to shave our monochromatic friend just here." He pointed with the scalpel.

"Mr. Pipes's *razor*?"

"You don't think I would use *my* razor," said Dr. Dudley, with a twirl of his moustache, "on a skunk?"

Annie hurried from the room and returned with the razor.

"And then I shall perform the incision along this curve," he continued, flourishing the scalpel.

"Carefully?"

"Most carefully, Annie, I assure you."

"Your job will be to keep any—ah—fluids," he said, "from obstructing my work. Now, then, shall we commence?"

Half an hour later, after stitching up the incision, Dr. Dudley led Annie into the Garden Room, where Mr. Pipes sat reading and Drew paced anxiously in front of the window.

"All is well?" asked Mr. Pipes.

"A most successful operation," said Dr. Dudley, "if I do say so myself."

"Monochrome's vital signs seem good," smiled Annie. "He's still sleeping, of course."

"*Monochrome?*" said Drew.

"You, know, like the film," said Annie. "Dr. Dudley says black and white film's called monochrome film; seems like a good name for a skunk, don't you think?"

"Now, I propose some fresh air out of doors," said Dr. Dudley. "We need to dispose of … er … something—and the greater the distance from the house, the better."

"So we've got to go skiing again," said Drew.

"Most certainly," said Dr. Dudley.

After they all climbed out the window, Mr. Pipes suggested leaving it open only a very small crack this time.

"We can ill-afford to take in all skunks in the neighborhood," said Mr. Pipes.

They buried the odor sac under a fir tree, digging as far down in the snow as they could with their skis.

"And now," said Dr. Dudley, "if I may propose a bit more ambitious skiing—sorry Mr. Pipes, only for the young and strong—down this magnificent hill."

"Oh, yeah," said Drew. "This one is a biggy."

Mr. Pipes frowned.

"You will of course," said Mr. Pipes, "be careful of that grove of trees positioned rather ominously half way down the—the precipice."

"Precipice! Ridiculous, my dear man," snorted Dr. Dudley. "A trifling mole hill for one of my expertise—a mere warm-up slope, I assure you."

"Perhaps," said Mr. Pipes. "But do think of the children."

"G-good idea," said Annie. "I like the other hill better."

"I *am* thinking of the children," Dr. Dudley called over his shoulder, pushing off with his poles and plunging forward down the steep hill. "When else will they have an opportunity to learn from such a skill—"

His voice suddenly fell away.

What happened next would be imprinted on Annie and Drew's minds—forever.

The Law of God Is Good and Wise

The precepts of the LORD are right, giving joy to the heart. The commands of the
LORD are radiant, giving light to the eyes. Ps. 19:8

1. The law of God is good and wise and sets his
2. Its light of ho - li - ness im - parts the
3. To those who help in Christ have found and would in
4. When men the of - fered help dis - dain and wil - ful -

will be - fore our eyes, shows us the way of
of our sin - ful hearts, that we may see our
works of love a - bound it shows what deeds are
ly in sin re - main, its ter - ror in their

righ - teous - ness, and dooms to death when we trans- gress.
lost es - tate and seek de - liv - 'rance ere too late.
his de - light and should be done as good and right.
ear re - sounds and keeps their wick - ed - ness in bounds.

5. The law is good; but since the fall
   its holiness condemns us all;
   it dooms us for our sin to die
   and has no pow'r to justify.

6. To Jesus we for refuge flee,
   who from the curse has set us free,
   and humbly worship at his throne,
   saved by his grace through faith alone.

Matthias Loy, 1863   ERHALT UNS, HERR L.M.
                                                      Geistliche Lieder, Wittenberg, 1543

Chapter Eleven

Horatio G. Spafford

1828–1888

When peace, like a river, attendeth my way,
When sorrows like sea billows roll;
Whatever my lot, Thou hast taught me to say;
It is well, it is well with my soul.

Horrified, Mr. Pipes and Annie and Drew watched Dr. Dudley as he veered to his left, desperately trying to avoid crashing into a tree. He missed the tree. Yet, in a sort of slow motion, he lost all control and went down in a cloud of powder. But then he resurfaced, feet and skis uppermost, rolling forward, his arms, poles, legs and skis splayed out like the sails of a windmill. In a frame-by-frame sequence, he repeated the feat over and over, coming up whiter and whiter with each revolution.

At the bottom of the hill he stopped. The powder settled.

"Dear Lord, preserve him," breathed Mr. Pipes.

Tears flowed down Annie's cold cheeks.

"I-is he alright?" she asked.

"I'm gonna go see," said Drew.

"Stop!" cried Mr. Pipes. "Drew, you go get the sled you saw in the woodshed. It is almost certain he will be unable to ski back—do be quick. Annie, work your way slowly and carefully in a series of gradual angles down the slope to Dr. Dudley."

With that, Mr. Pipes sidestepped his way with his snowshoes down the slope until puffing with exertion he came alongside the prone figure. Annie soon joined him.

"Well, then," began Mr. Pipes, soothingly, "how are you feeling?" He wiped snow away from Dr. Dudley's face. "Tell me, dear man, where are you hurt?"

Dr. Dudley lifted a snow-covered arm slightly, dropped it and groaned.

"Where—" he gasped, "where, do I *not* hurt—" He winced in pain and reached for his left knee. "It would require much less effort if you asked me where I do not hurt—perhaps no effort at all."

"Keep quiet then," said Mr. Pipes. "Drew has gone for the sled—we shall get you to a doctor as quickly as we can."

"I *am* a doctor," retorted Dr. Dudley.

"Yes, yes, I know," said Mr. Pipes.

"And because I *am* a doctor," he continued, "I know that my leg is almost certainly broken."

Annie looked on wide-eyed and speechless.

◈ ◈ ◈

Ten minutes later, Drew arrived on his skis, pulling the sled behind him with the rope Dr. Dudley had the foresight to purchase.

"I brought along a sleeping bag," he said, breathing hard. "And the caretaker telephoned the Amesbury Health Center to let them know we'd be coming."

"Good work, Drew," said Mr. Pipes. "Now, Annie and Drew, help me scoot him onto the sled—gently, now, and together—lift!"

Mr. Pipes then unlaced Dr. Dudley's ski boots and they wrapped the sleeping bag around him. Drew lashed Dr. Dudley onto the sled with one end of the rope while Mr. Pipes tied on the ski boots and stepped into Dr. Dudley's skis.

"I shall tie myself in the middle," said Mr. Pipes. "Annie, you on my left and Drew tie in on the right; we shall achieve the most even pull for the trek to the health center. Is everyone ready?"

"You're not—" gasped Dr. Dudley, "skiing, are you, Mr. Pipes?"

"Brittle-boned though I am, I am most certainly skiing," replied Mr. Pipes simply.

"I trust you will be careful," said Dr. Dudley, faintly as the sled moved forward over the snow.

Both Annie and Drew couldn't help feeling something of the excitement of a winter snow rescue. It was just too bad that in order to have a rescue, Annie mused, someone had to get hurt.

"Keep him level," said Mr. Pipes as they approached a drift on the still-unplowed street.

"Do listen to him, children," came Dr. Dudley's voice from the sled.

"The health center's just around the corner," said Drew.

"Does it hurt lots?" asked Annie.

"Hurt? Naturally you would not be expected to know how I suffer," replied Dr. Dudley, "my bearing all in silence."

Once inside the health center, the no-nonsense New England nurses and doctors had Dr. Dudley examined, x-rayed, repaired and in a clean white-sheeted bed with an efficiency that left Dr. Dudley speechless. The morphine they gave him for pain no doubt had something to do with his tranquility.

❖ ❖ ❖

An hour later, Mr. Pipes looked out the window of the health center as the sun set and shadows fell on the snow.

Dr. Dudley stirred, blinked rapidly and looked at them in some confusion.

"I say," he said, "For what are you all standing around mouth a gape?"

The three looked at each other.

"You must get off home—well, to Mr. Whittier's house—at once. Monochrome will be awake; he will need you all. Now, off you go. I believe I shall be in very good hands." He smiled at a row of white-frocked admirers enamored with his accent and awaiting his command.

"The skunk!" said Drew.

"I'd almost forgotten him," said Annie.

"You will be all right without us?" asked Mr. Pipes.

"Go, of course I will," said Dr. Dudley, "but I am concerned for Monochrome—poor chap'll be beside himself just awakening from surgery as he has." Then dismissing them with his hand, and turning to his nurses, he said, "Ladies, how about a pot of tea? Let me explain how it should be brewed...."

⊠ ⊠ ⊠

The moon rose and shone brilliantly off the drifted snow as they skied back to the edge of town and Mr. Whittier's house. All was silent except the crunch and glide of their skis. Eager as she was to get back to Monochrome, Annie fell behind because she kept pausing to admire the white muted moonlight casting bulging and softly rippling shadows along the snow. Everything glowed with mystery and beauty and she just had to stop.

"It looks like an enormous soft, fluffy blanket," said Annie after she caught up again. "And it's covering sleeping giants."

"Hmm," said Mr. Pipes.

"You see, that over there is a giant shoulder—and that's his head. And see, he's got his arms crossed under the covers."

"And those are his feet," said Drew. "Or is that Dr. Dudley's pickup?"

They laughed.

"It is more lovely than words can describe," said Mr. Pipes as they took their skis off at the back window.

"What a great way to spend Christmas Eve," said Drew, his cheeks red and his breath lingering in little clouds before disappearing into the still night. "Now if we could figure out some way to go fishing."

"But poor Dr. Dudley," said Annie.

"We must ring your parents and tell them what has happened," said Mr. Pipes. "I fear, that even if the roads open tomorrow—"

"That's Christmas Day," said Annie, biting her lower lip.

"Yes, it is." Mr. Pipes looked sympathetically at Annie in the moonlight. "We simply cannot leave Dr. Dudley."

"I know," said Annie.

"I think he's fine," said Drew. "In fact, I think he likes it all."
Mr. Pipes just smiled.

◈ ◈ ◈

Once inside, Mr. Pipes had Drew get a snow shovel from the
summer kitchen to dig out the front door. While Drew worked,
Annie ran to the kitchen to check on Monochrome. Her heart
skipped a beat when she first saw him lying in the little wood box
near the stove. But then she put her hand on his black and white
coat; his tiny heart beat steadily—tink-tink, tink-tink. She studied his face: he's smiling in his sleep, she decided. Annie stroked
his coarse fur; he gave a little sigh.

Mr. Pipes crouched before the fireplace, blowing and stoking
the coals back to life. Drew knocked on the front door and Mr.
Pipes and Annie, with much grunting and pushing and pulling,
let him in.

"Whew!" he said, wiping his forehead. "That's like work."

"Nice job, Drew," said Mr. Pipes. "Now we can come and go
more easily."

Drew pulled his coat off. "And how's Monochrome?"

"He's still resting," said Annie.

"Resting in peace?" asked Drew.

"He's not dead, if that's what you mean," said Annie. "He
even smiled."

They all went into the kitchen and checked on the skunk.

"I think he will be fine," said Mr. Pipes, patting the little animal. "Dr. Dudley is a first-rate surgeon—I am repeatedly told."

Mr. Pipes put a telephone call through to Annie and Drew's
parents in California. Annie swallowed and blinked rapidly while
she talked to her mother. Then Mr. Pipes conversed with their
parents in low tones for several minutes before saying good-bye
and putting down the receiver.

What Annie and Drew did not hear went like this:

"The children's father and I could never live with ourselves—
what parent could?—if we didn't spend Christmas with our children."

"I am so terribly sorry—" began Mr. Pipes.

"Oh, we don't blame you," replied their mother. "What could you do about any of it?"

"Nevertheless, madam—" began Mr. Pipes again.

"Well, it's like no way we can have Christmas without our children."

"I only wish there was something I—"

"There isn't," she cut him off. "But, we have a plan. According to our latest information, the storm is over and flights are coming in and out of Boston no problem. Bill's rescheduled his appointments and we're flying out—tonight. That should put us there—Christmas Day."

"The children will be most—"

"So how was it you get to Amesbury from Boston?"

"Perhaps the trains will be—"

"Never mind, we'll figure that out. But listen, don't say anything to the children; it'll be our surprise."

During this conversation Annie busied herself by putting the kettle on, and while it heated she sorted through Dr. Dudley's ample provisions. Moments later, she returned to the Garden Room balancing a tray crowded with the teapot and several varieties of candies and cookies. Drew's mouth watered as he devoured with his eyes a tin of chocolate-covered hard caramels decorated with slivered almonds.

They munched and sipped in silence before the fire.

"Now, all we need is some music," said Drew. "It's Christmas Eve. I wish this place had a CD player or a piano or something."

"An organ would be nice,' said Annie.

"Indeed, it would," laughed Mr. Pipes. "Though highly unlikely."

"Yeah, Mr. Whittier feeling the way he did about organs," said Drew.

"We can sing without all that," said Annie. "Mr. Pipes, let's sing carols!"

Whittier's house rang with joyful singing celebrating the birth of the Lord Jesus. They sang until they had to stop and rest their voices.

"What would the world be like without great singing!" said Annie, her eyes sparkling with happiness.

"I'm not sure ours was so great," said Drew.

"I mean the carols and the hymns you've taught us, Mr. Pipes," said Annie. "Those are great."

"Oh, indeed they are," replied Mr. Pipes.

Drew drained his tea mug.

"What makes one hymn a great one," he asked, "and another just a song—not great at all?"

Mr. Pipes was silent for a moment.

"A most important question, Drew," replied Mr. Pipes.

"A great hymn, that is worthy of being offered to God in worship," began Mr. Pipes, "must be true theologically—that is, it must have doctrinal substance, filled with solid statements of the objective reasons for praise. It must also give us accurate words expressive of the way things really are in life; and it must be passionate poetry of the highest order.

"There is another feature evident in the great hymns. Do you know what it might be?" inquired Mr. Pipes.

"They lead us from ourselves to God?" suggested Annie.

"Well said, and a most critical test of greatness," replied Mr. Pipes. "Another way of putting it is to say that the point of view in our praise must be God-ward, that is it must fix our minds on God—on His person and works more than on our subjective experience of Him."

"I think I understand," said Drew a little hesitantly. "So, maybe 'Free From the Law, O Happy Condition,' puts more emphasis on my happiness than on God's holiness. Is that what you mean?"

"Yes, that among its other problems," replied Mr. Pipes. "I fear to tell you, my dears, that American singing in church in the nineteenth and twentieth centuries was filled with a sentimental spirituality, devoid of doctrine and much more interested in superficial experience than in rejoicing with trembling before the God of the Universe."

He paused and stared into the fire for several minutes before continuing.

"Do understand, I am not criticizing merely for the sake of criticizing. Americans in the 1800s, though often sentimental, were progressive and confident—almost proud at times, and this deeply affected the way in which Christians sang to God."

"Like how?" said Drew.

"One fellow wrote a rousing song, the goal of which was to call men to rise up and be great by serving in the church."

"That seems a bit turned around," said Drew.

"Indeed," said Mr. Pipes. "Many of the songs were sincere evangelistic songs with catchy tunes suited to be sung at camp meetings and designed to draw in the unbelievers of that day. They employed repeated refrains—often sung many times over. Perhaps the first line of one of them speaks for them all: 'Sing them over again to me,' followed by the phrase 'Wonderful words of life.' This they sang over and over again to music that I can only describe as music suited to the carousel—toy horses rising and falling, in a fixed posture of great vigor, but merely following the leader going happily in circles."

"How did it sound?" asked Drew.

Mr. Pipes frowned as he hummed the tune.

"That sounds like roller-skating music," said Annie.

"Yeah, or the seventh-inning stretch music at a baseball game," added Drew.

"But it doesn't sound like music to worship God with," said Annie.

"Remember what Mr. Luther said?" asked Mr. Pipes, looking from one to the other intently."

"Wasn't it, 'We need poets!'" said Annie.

"Precisely," said Mr. Pipes. "And we need musicians! Drew and Annie, you must perfect your gifts and add deep and timeless hymns—poetry and music—to the church's worship."

"This stuff doesn't seem to help you think," said Drew.

"I fear," said Mr. Pipes, "thinking had little to do with this sort of singing. When sentimentalism takes hold of the church, men have less and less appetite for thinking. Consider the gospel song, 'In the Garden,' ranked the second most favorite by American Christians in the mid-twentieth century; it illustrates the emptiness of sentimentalism and, alas, how pervasive that sentimentalism was. Based on Mary's encounter with Jesus on Resurrection Sunday, it fabricates an emotional effect completely foreign to Psalm-like devotion. What is more, it forces the one singing to put himself in an impossible situation. 'I come to the garden alone, while the dew is still on the roses …' it begins. None of us can say that honestly. But then we are forced to sing over and again in the refrain the absurd sentiment: 'And the joy we share as we tarry there, None other has ever known.'"

"Wait a second," said Drew. "If a whole congregation of Christians sings that together—how can it mean anything? 'None other has ever known!' that's kind of ridiculous."

"I think John Eliot would call that 'froth,'" said Annie.

"Yes," agreed Mr. Pipes. "This kind of singing gave the worshipper a sort of vague sense of well-being, which gave the dull sort of assumption to many that their walk with the Lord was greater than anyone else's. Some might argue that this kind of sentiment led to the spiritual mediocrity of this generation."

"But Christians then were sincere, weren't they?" asked Annie. "I mean, they meant well, didn't they?"

"Oh, indeed," said Mr. Pipes, "sincerity is the relatively easy part. But we can never use that fact as reason for accepting mediocrity or worse yet, for allowing false doctrine or shallow devotion to tarnish our praise."

"So, after Mr. Loy, or Mr. Palmer," said Annie, "wasn't anyone writing good hymns in America?"

"Well, there was the Chicago lawyer, Horatio Spafford," said Mr. Pipes, "who wrote an anguished but confident gospel song of considerable quality."

"Why anguished?" asked Annie.

Mr. Pipes sighed. "You remember how I told you that hymn stories sometimes get twisted about and spiced up, as it were, to make them more sensational?"

"Yes," they both remembered.

"Well, there are about as many versions of this story as there are—" he looked at Drew, "—as there are fast food restaurants in America!"

"Which one's true?" asked Annie.

"I shall give you the one that seems best suited to the evidence. In 1874 the French passenger ship, *Ville du Havre*, steamed toward Europe across the Atlantic. Situated comfortably on board were Mrs. Spafford and her four children coming to England on holiday. In mid ocean the steamer collided with a sailing vessel and sank in half an hour—nearly everyone drowned. However, a sailor rowing a lifeboat over the wreckage found Mrs. Spafford—barely alive."

"A-and the children?" asked Annie.

"All lost, my dear, all lost," said Mr. Pipes.

"When she arrived in Cardiff, Wales," he continued, "she cabled her husband just two words: 'Saved alone.'"

"I can't imagine it," said Drew quietly.

"Poor man; he'd be so glad his wife was saved," said Annie. "But then so sad about his children. It must have been awful."

"Mixed emotions, of the very highest order, no doubt," said Mr. Pipes. "Some time later, after his wife rejoined him in Chicago, and while D. L. Moody and Ira Sankey visited the couple, Mr. Spafford wrote a hymn in memory of his dear children lost at sea. One account—no doubt too good to be true—has him going to sea and stopping right over the spot where his children were lost. And whilst looking out on the vast ocean that swallowed up his little ones, penning the words, 'When peace like a river attendeth my way,' known by a phrase in the chorus, 'It is Well With My Soul.'

"However it was written, Spafford's memorial hymn expresses trust in God's goodness and sovereignty—good poetry, it is, enriched and strengthened by the anguish of the poet."

They sang softly with Mr. Pipes:

> When peace like a river, attendeth my way,
> When sorrows like sea billows roll;
> Whatever my lot, Thou hast taught me to say,
> It is well, it is well with my soul.

> Though Satan should buffet, though trials should come,
> Let this blessed assurance control,
> That Christ has regarded my helpless estate,
> And has shed His own blood for my soul.

> My sin—O the bliss of this glorious thought—
> My sin, not in part, but the whole,
> Is nailed to the cross and I bear it no more;
> Praise the Lord, praise the Lord, O my soul!

> O Lord, haste the day when the faith shall be sight,
> The clouds be rolled back as a scroll,
> The trump shall resound and the Lord shall descend;
> "Even so"—it is well with my soul.

Annie leaned on Mr. Pipes's shoulder and gazed at the hymnal.

"'When sorrows like sea billows roll,'" she read aloud softly. "You can hear his grief in these lines—but there's something else."

Drew scanned down the lines again.

"Hope," he said simply.

"Yes, and many have found that hope," said Mr. Pipes, "while singing these words in the midst of great loss."

Drew got up and a moment later returned with a load of split logs in his arms.

"It is time we turn in for the night," said Mr. Pipes. Annie thought she detected a twinkle in his eye as he added, "Tomorrow is Christmas!"

They checked on Monochrome.

"He's still asleep," said Annie, sounding disappointed. "Can I bring his box into my room tonight?"

"I don't see why not," replied Mr. Pipes.

"Is he ever going to wake up?" asked Drew skeptically.

"At best he'd be dormant this time of year," said Mr. Pipes. "But what with surgery and all, it's no wonder he sleeps on. Let him rest. Perhaps he'll join us tomorrow for Christmas dinner!"

"But what about Dr. Dudley?" asked Annie.

"Yeah, will he have to eat hospital food for Christmas dinner?" asked Drew.

"I believe Dr. Dudley will fare very well indeed at the health center," said Mr. Pipes. "Though perhaps a visit to him in the morning might be in order."

"On skis?" asked Drew.

"They've plowed only main roads," said Mr. Pipes. "We must ski."

"Do you think they'd let me bring Monochrome in to see Dr. Dudley?" asked Annie.

"Hmm, a sort of post-operative visit?" said Mr. Pipes.

"Oh, yes," said Annie.

"One can only try."

Too tired for writing poetry that night, Annie drifted toward sleep, her hand reaching down and stroking Monochrome snuggled in his box on the floor next to her bed. What a day it had been! And tomorrow was Christmas—she sighed heavily. She and Drew had never been away from home on Christmas before.

It Is Well with My Soul

The peace of God, which transcends all understanding, will guard your hearts
and your minds in Christ Jesus. Phil. 4:7

1. When peace, like a riv - er, at - tend - eth my way, when sor - rows like
2. Though Sa - tan should buf - fet, though tri - als should come, let this blest as -
3. My sin— O the bliss of this glo - ri- ous thought!—my sin, not in
4. O Lord, haste the day when the faith shall be sight, the clouds be rolled

sea bil - lows roll; what - ev - er my lot, thou hast taught me to say,
sur - ance con - trol, that Christ has re - gard - ed my help - less es - tate,
part, but the whole, is nailed to the cross and I bear it no more;
back as a scroll, the trump shall re - sound and the Lord shall de - scend,

REFRAIN

"It is well, it is well with my soul."
and has shed his own blood for my soul. It is well
praise the Lord, praise the Lord, O my soul! It is well
"E - ven so"— it is well with my soul.

with my soul; it is well, it is well with my soul.
with my soul;

Horatio G. Spafford, 1873

VILLE DU HAVRE 11.8.11.9.ref.
Philip P. Bliss, 1876

Chapter Twelve

Winter and Christmas!

Popular Praise & Historic Christian Worship

I need you to hold me
Like my daddy never could.
And I need you to show me
How resting in your arms can be so good.

—Or—

Fatherlike He tends and spares us;
Well our feeble frame He knows;
In His arms He gently bears us,
Rescues us from all our foes;
Praise Him, praise Him,
Praise Him, praise Him,
Widely as His mercy goes.

Henry Francis Lyte

After yesterday's accident and the late night, Annie felt herself emerging far too early in the morning from the dullness of sleep. She sniffed then scratched at her nose and sniffed again. Something was tickling her nose!

Without opening her eyes she said in a sleepy voice, "Knock it off, please, Drew." Feathers, probably; he was always collecting feathers.

In response, she heard a sort of snuffling breathing in her face. She opened her eyes wide. Staring back at her were two dark eyes set in a black and white furry face, tiny moist nostrils flared as they took in her scent.

"Monochrome! You're awake!" she squealed softly, stroking the young skunk under his chin.

Sunlight shone brilliantly off the snow through her window. She hopped up and dressed. Then, scooping Monochrome up in her arms she headed for the kitchen.

"Merry Christmas!" boomed Mr. Pipes cheerfully from the stove. "Oh, and what have we here?"

"Merry Christmas to you, too!" said Annie.

"So he woke up," said Drew, between mouthfuls of cold cereal and milk.

"Yeah," said Annie, smiling at her skunk. "You wanted to have Christmas with us didn't you, you cute little thing, you— Oh, Oocheepoo. And he crawled in bed with me. In fact, I thought you were tickling me, Drew, but it was Monochrome— whispering in my ear. Oh, you're the sweetest thing I've ever seen!" She gave him a gentle squeeze.

"Annie, you're embarrassing me," said Drew.

Mr. Pipes smiled.

"Drew is having an appetizer," he said, pouring boiling water into the teapot, "before Christmas breakfast—bacon, eggs, pancakes with maple syrup, all prepared just as you like them."

"Hurrah!"

"Hurrah!"

"Then I thought we would strap on our skis and go to the health center and wish Dr. Dudley a Merry Christmas."

"What about a tree?" asked Drew. "We sort of need a Christmas tree, don't we?"

"I took the liberty of speaking with the caretaker about just that matter," said Mr. Pipes. "She has graciously loaned us a potted Norfolk pine from her indoor plant collection. The lovely little thing is in the Garden Room. Perhaps, after our visit to the health center you would help me decorate it?"

Annie and Drew rushed out of the kitchen to inspect the tree.

"It's lovely and it's almost as tall as Drew," said Annie, coming back into the kitchen. For a fleeting moment she felt a wave of sadness; this would be the first Christmas she could remember not decorating the tree with their mother.

"But now for breakfast," said Mr. Pipes, followed by a loud sizzling as he ladled pancake batter onto the frying pan.

⊠ ⊠ ⊠

"I don't think I've ever seen the sky such a deep, deep blue," said Annie, as they skied alongside the newly plowed street on their way to the health center. She adjusted the straps on her knapsack.

Mr. Pipes smiled at the frosted brick houses and trees laden with mounds of snow along the street. With squeals and laughter, rosy-cheeked children, making a snowman in their yard, halted and pitched snowballs at them. Mr. Pipes and Annie and Drew called out season's greetings to a family skiing past across the street.

"This will be a Christmas to remember," said Mr. Pipes, his cheeks pink with exertion and the crisp air.

At the next cross street, Drew stopped and read a sign with an arrow pointing left.

"'Lake Carter, $\frac{1}{2}$ mile,'" he read, with excitement. "I wonder if there's any fish in it."

"It would be strictly ice fishing, at present," said Mr. Pipes.

"Fishing for ice?" said Drew.

Mr. Pipes laughed. "No, no, my boy. Fishing *through* ice. I'm told it's very good sport, though a bit on the chilly side."

Annie halted in her tracks. The bulges in her knapsack kept wiggling. "It's okay, Monochrome," she cooed over her shoulder. "We'll be there in a minute; have another cracker."

A black pointy nose poked out of the knapsack flap and for a brief moment looked around curiously at the snow. Monochrome disappeared into the knapsack and the sound of contented crunching came from inside.

⊠ ⊠ ⊠

"There now, imagine it," said Dr. Dudley, his leg shrouded in a fresh plaster cast and suspended in the air by a chain. "My friends have not forgotten me."

"Merry Christmas!" they said together.

"How are you, my dear fellow," asked Mr. Pipes.

"Fine, oh, fine, indeed," said Dr. Dudley. "Barring the fact that it is Christmas and I am trussed up with a broken leg and cannot leave for who knows how long. No, I am fine indeed."

"We who saw it, thank the Lord you are not hurt more seriously after such a fall," said Mr. Pipes.

"Yes, well, I bear all patiently," said Dr. Dudley. "Now, then, how is my patient?"

"Monochrome is wonderful," said Annie, "like nothing ever happened. Do you want to see him?"

"Rather!" snorted Dr. Dudley. "But you torment me, it is, of course, impossible." He turned to the wall.

Smiling, Annie sat down on the edge of his bed and opened her knapsack. Out waddled Monochrome onto Dr. Dudley's lap. He snuffled at the remains of Dr. Dudley's breakfast pushed aside on a tray.

"I say!" said Dr. Dudley, brightening. "I say, I say!"

He stroked the coarse fur and with grunts and *oohs* and *ahs* of admiration at his work, he inspected the little creature.

"He's fit as a fiddle!"

"And no more stink for this skunk," said Drew.

"You have done fine surgery on him," said Mr. Pipes. "I would trust my health in your hands without reservation."

Just then they heard a quick knock on the door and in bustled a smiling nurse balancing a tray of instruments in her hands.

"Greetings to our English doctor patient," she called cheerfully, not yet spotting Monochrome. "Now, you behave yourself while I give you a little poke and check your blood—"

She broke off. Her eyes bulged and she threw her hand over her mouth stifling what would have been a blood-curdling scream. The tray crashed to the floor. Monochrome arched his back and unfurled his fuzzy black and white tail. Everyone held his breath.

"Oh, oh, i-i-it's going to—" stammered the nurse, fanning the air with one hand and gripping her nose with the other.

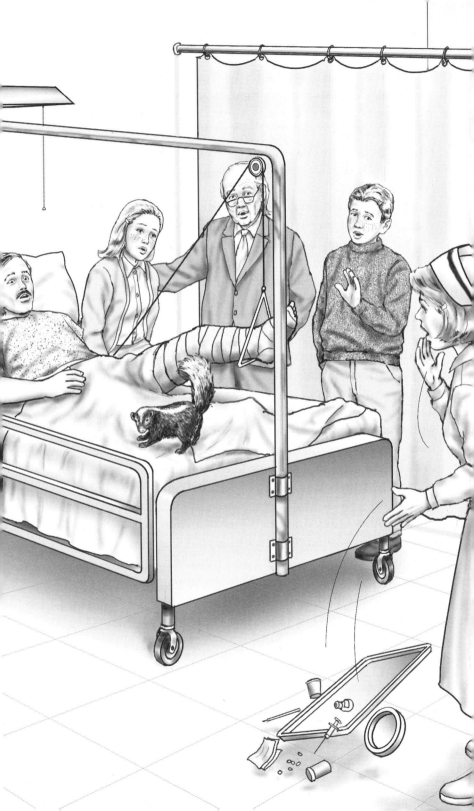

Annie and Drew looked at Dr. Dudley, the little skunk poised on his lap. For a moment they thought he looked worried. What would happen if Monochrome's surgery didn't actually work?

"My dear nurse," said Dr. Dudley. "There is no odor, for I have surgically removed Monochrome's odor sac."

The nurse shook her head and kept her fingers pinched tightly on her nose.

"My dear, there is no foul odor," insisted Dr. Dudley, taking a deep and noisy breath in an attempt to prove it.

"Ge' i' ou' of my hospi'al!" she insisted, pointing at the door, her nose still plugged.

Mr. Pipes, Annie, Monochrome, and Drew beat a hasty retreat, wishing Dr. Dudley a Merry Christmas.

⬛ ⬛ ⬛

Back at Mr. Whittier's house, Annie and Drew made cut-out angels, stars, sheep, and mangers out of colored paper given them by the caretaker. They popped corn—"Like the Indians used to do," explained Drew—and showed Mr. Pipes how to stitch it with needle and thread into stringers to drape around the little tree. They arranged candles in rows along the mantle and table to be lit that evening. The house filled with the delicious smells of roasting ham, baking sweet potatoes and simmering cranberries.

When they finished decorating the tree, Annie prepared a pot of tea and laid out shortbread Christmas cookies shimmering with frosting and flecked with colored sprinkles. Drew brought in an armload of logs and they sat down for morning tea before the cheery warmth of the fire.

"Merry Christmas to us all!" said Mr. Pipes, then sipping his tea.

"My gift for you," said Annie sadly, "is at home."

"So's mine," said Drew. "All of our gifts are at home."

"That we are here together,' said Mr. Pipes, "is gift enough. But, I just happen to have a little something I've brought for each of you, my dears."

"What?" asked Drew eagerly.

Annie frowned at her brother.

Mr. Pipes handed each of them a neatly wrapped parcel. Drew said thanks and tore into his.

"Well, go on," said Mr. Pipes to Annie.

In each of their boxes they found a little leather case with two gold pens, one a fountain pen and the other a ball-point. Mr. Pipes had engraved their names on each pen. Digging further down into the rustling tissue paper, they both found a beautiful leather-bound book. They opened them eagerly.

Drew looked at Mr. Pipes in surprise.

"There's nothing in mine!" he said.

"Oh, it's such beautiful leather," said Annie, running her hand over the calf binding. "But mine's blank, too."

"Precisely," said Mr. Pipes, smiling at them. "They are extra thick and *you* are to fill them—fill them with poetry and music written in praise of God."

"Oh, thank you, Mr. Pipes," they said together.

"Now, dig just a bit further," said Mr. Pipes.

"Giant chocolate bars!" exclaimed Drew.

"English chocolate," said Annie.

"Watch yours closely, Annie," said Mr. Pipes, eyeing Drew, who had already torn into his wrapper.

◈ ◈ ◈

Annie opened her old sketchbook on the desktop and reread her versification of Psalm 86. She sighed. It was Christmas; she was happy here with Mr. Pipes and her brother—and Monochrome. And she'd just decided not to think about not spending Christmas with their parents, not to think about it at all … no, not at all.

Mr. Pipes studied Annie's face as he offered her another cookie.

"We need some Christmas cheer," he said. "Annie, what carol would you have us sing for you?"

"Mr. Watts," said Annie, brightening a little.

"'Joy to the World,' it is," said Mr. Pipes. They lifted their voices together in praise: "'... Let earth receive her King!'"

"And, how about Mr. Brooks?" suggested Drew, when they finished: "'O, little town of Bethlehem....'"

And on and on they sang.

Then Mr. Pipes read from the Christmas story in Matthew: "... [S]he was found with child by the Holy Spirit.... She will give birth to a son, and you are to give him the name Jesus, because he will save his people from their sins ... and they will call him Immanuel—which means, 'God with us.'"

"It's amazing," said Drew, studying a wisp of smoke curling up into the chimney. "Jesus could be a little baby born to poor parents in a barn—and at the same time be God."

"Yes, it is amazing," said Mr. Pipes.

Annie pulled her knees up under her chin.

"Do you think he cried?" she asked.

"Cried?" said Mr. Pipes.

"Jesus, when He was a baby," said Annie. "Do you think even though He was God that He cried?"

"Ah," said Mr. Pipes, smiling at her. "You are thinking of the phrase from 'Away in a Manger,' are you not?"

"'No crying he makes,'" said Annie. "I'm not sure that's true. What do you think, Mr. Pipes?"

"Perhaps an instance of sentimentalism," replied Mr. Pipes. "Jesus was a real man—'in all points tempted like as we are, yet without sin.' I am most certain that as a baby he cried—not in fits and tantrums, mind you—but in discomfort and the like, he would have cried like any other real baby."

"It's sort of a balance then," said Drew.

"Balance?" said Mr. Pipes.

"Yeah, between our thinking of Him as a real child and as God."

Mr. Pipes sighed and rubbed his hand across his chin before replying.

"It's kind of like that when we worship God," said Annie. "He's God, the Creator, the King of kings and He's all powerful, on the one hand. But on the other, he's more gentle, like a Shepherd. How do we keep all this straight?"

"And doesn't the Bible call us children of God," said Drew. "And if Jesus was God's Son (a son's a child)—then, hey, that makes Jesus our brother!"

"To be sure, my dears," began Mr. Pipes, "there is familiarity in man's address to God in Scripture—'The Lord is my Shepherd …' and we call God 'Abba Father,' or 'Daddy.' But many today prefer the familiar dimension of God's being and have little taste for His transcendence."

"What does transcendence mean?" asked Drew.

"It means that God is high above us, that we are His creatures and He is the Holy, Almighty God Who made and rules the universe at His will."

Annie cradled her chin in her hands and frowned.

"We sing what Mother calls 'ditties' at church with the Smiths," said Annie. "She likes us singing those better than the hymns you teach us. I'm not sure why."

"She calls your hymns, 'dirges,'" said Drew.

"I like the hymns, but they do take more work to sing—and understand," said Annie.

"Yeah, they're way better," said Drew. "You know, you can't really sing the praise choruses loud," he went on, "like you can with 'Glorious Things of Thee are Spoken,' or lots of the others. I can sing those loud."

"Why is that?" asked Mr. Pipes.

"Well, with the choruses you sort of have to squint your eyes closed and sway from side to side," said Drew, demonstrating. "And it gets kind of mushy—lots of the girls like 'em, but most of the boys just mumble along and feel kind of uncomfortable."

"But lots of people who sing praise choruses," said Annie, "really do love Jesus—the songs are all about a close relationship with Jesus—most of them."

"I don't entirely doubt that, Annie," said Mr. Pipes. "But, alas, the praise choruses of the postmodern church often feature a vague sort of relationship—a familiarity based on rather elastic sorts of notions about God—ones that can be stretched and pulled to fit in with popular ideas. Hold a great hymn of Ray Palmer, for example, up next to a praise chorus and you will observe several important differences."

"Like what?" asked Annie.

"The timeless hymns of the church are full of the reasons for our sung devotion to God. Praise choruses contain less and less doctrine so the praise springs not from clearly stated truths about God, His person and works, but from an ill-defined feeling of love and adoration. And the one doing the singing is much more the focus of consideration in most praise choruses than God, the stated object of the praise."

"What do you mean?" asked Annie.

"Well, typical first lines of postmodern praise singing illustrate my point best: 'I bless You,' 'I only want to love You,' and 'I just want to praise You.' What we are doing and hoping to get out of this kind of singing seems much more important than the more difficult work of extolling the attributes and works of our Lord in a more Psalm-like manner."

"But lots of the praise choruses are straight from Scripture," said Annie, "even from the Psalms. How can there be anything wrong with those?"

"One must look at the bigger picture of what is happening in the church. The Psalms have been sung for thousands of years, but there is an important and disturbing difference between the Psalm singing of historic Christianity and today's singing of portions of the Psalms."

"How is it different?" asked Drew.

"Christian musicians today edit out the more complex doctrinal portions of Psalms and merely leave the praising bit in—now with fewer, if any, reasons stated for that praise. The simplest parts of Psalms are sung today—usually sung over and over again creating a warm but often only vague feeling of adoration."

"So is feeling ... *bad* in worship?" asked Annie.

"By no means," replied Mr. Pipes. "The Psalms and the hymns of the church are full of deep emotion and heart-felt praise. But that spiritual feeling always follows objective doctrinal truth adorned in the poetry. The church today has an insatiable appetite for the religious feelings hoped for in worship but virtually no appetite for the theological content that must come first and inform the experience of God's presence in our worship."

"It's sort of like you can't get there from here," said Drew. "You can't have real feeling without the reasons for the feelings, right?"

"Precisely," said Mr. Pipes.

"Mr. Palmer's hymn, 'Lord, My Weak Thought in Vain Would Climb,' is a good example of what is not happening in worship today. Few want to lift weak thoughts to greater heights of understanding leading to true praise; why should they, when it is so much easier to have feelings created by popular mood music and simplistic words. It's hard work thinking about the high truths of which Scriptural praise is so richly filled."

"But choruses are okay for kids, aren't they?" asked Annie.

"Ah, yes; an argument often insisted upon in their defense," said Mr. Pipes. "But let me ask you: at the Smiths' church, are these choruses sung only by the young? Or by adults as well?"

"That's a good point," said Annie. "They sing hardly any hymns—real hymns. It's everybody, kids and adults, singing mostly choruses in church."

"It is a striking thing, is it not, that with all the emphasis of Holy Scripture on children that God did not include a junior Psalter in the Bible from which generations of Jewish children might have sung simple tunes."

"That would seem kind of silly," said Annie.

"But alas," said Mr. Pipes, "that is what the church has done today—made a junior Psalter, in which the message is altered to be simplistic and easy. And I fear many sincere Christian adults will offer only this juvenile singing to God all their lives—'even down to old age.' That is a great pity."

"They're missing out on the best," said Drew.

"All the while thinking they've got it," added Mr. Pipes sadly.

"Most Christians actually think," he went on, "that today's praise choruses are a great improvement over the sung worship of the church in the past—perhaps they are somewhat better than the more recent past."

"If they only knew," said Annie.

"Employing the most up-to-date popular expressions of praise," said Mr. Pipes, "can tend to give people a sense of spiritual superiority over those who are considered to be *not with it*— I believe that is the accepted slang for being contemporary and up to fashion."

"Well, Mr. Pipes," said Drew, smiling, "you are definitely— *not with it!*"

"Thank you, my boy," said Mr. Pipes, touching his fingers to his forehead in salute. "I want for you, my dear ones, to bind yourselves with the church throughout the ages by singing with her what is timeless and enduring, not what is fashionable, predictable and thus, eminently disposable. Generations from now Christians will not find light in 'Shine, Jesus, Shine,' I assure you. Nor will composers of great music in future generations borrow praise chorus tunes—or should I say, tune."

"Most of them are pretty much the same," admitted Drew, "over and over."

"But none of this means that you and I have nothing to add to the canon of Christian hymnody, my dears," said Mr. Pipes.

Annie looked down at her sketchbook and the new lines she had been scribbling. She just couldn't bring herself to scribble on the clean white pages of her new leather writing book—not yet.

"You must contribute to the church throughout the ages," he continued, "by adding hymns and melodies of the highest quality, adorning the timeless truths of Holy Scripture and lifting high the cross of our Lord Jesus—Whose birthday it is!"

"And I smell dinner!" said Drew, licking his lips and rubbing his stomach.

◈   ◈   ◈

Mr. Pipes looked at his watch and strode casually into the parlor to look out the front window.

"What are you looking for?" asked Annie, cradling Monochrome in her arms.

Mr. Pipes smiled at Annie. "It is a lovely day for Christmas, isn't it, my dear?"

"Yes," replied Annie, blinking out the frosty windows.

"Shall we set the table and finish our dinner preparations?" he asked, his eyes twinkling merrily.

Annie smiled and followed him into the kitchen. She took down three plates from the cupboard and began setting the table.

"Only three plates?" said Mr. Pipes, his eyebrows aloft.

"I get to set one for Monochrome?" asked Annie eagerly.

"Well, my dear that is not exactly what I had in mind," said Mr. Pipes, laughing. "It's his manners; I fear the table would become a shambles."

"But Dr. Dudley's at the hospital," said Annie, looking puzzled. "That leaves only the three of us—at the table." She reached down and patted Monochrome sniffing along at her heels.

"It does?" said the old man, his eyes sparkling.

"What's he got up his sleeve?" said Drew.

Just then from the front of the house came the blaring of a horn. Drew and Annie bolted into the parlor.

"It's a snowplow!" said Drew. "And it's stopped right in front of the house."

Annie watched as the passenger door opened. She caught her breath and squealed with delight.

"It's Mom and Dad!" said Drew. "All the way out here! I can't believe it!"

Mr. Pipes smiled at their side.

"You knew all along!" said Annie.

"Not all along," said Mr. Pipes.

◈ ◈ ◈

Once in the front door, hugs, kisses, and handshakes were exchanged all around. Annie's mother recovered herself quickly af-

ter seeing Monochrome and said, "Skunks are people, too."
Their stepfather shook hands warmly with Mr. Pipes, comment-
ed on how primitive the house was, and asked what smelled so
good. The children's parents explained how the train line from
Boston deposited them only a few blocks from Mr. Whittier's
house, and how they were able to hitch a ride with the snowplow
right to the front door.

"Annie, you'd better put on two more plates," said Mr. Pipes.
"Dinner is served right this way." He led them to the table. Annie
took a lit candle from the mantle and soon the table glowed with
warm shimmering light as she lit a row of white candles. Drew
added a log to the fire in the dining room.

When the last chair legs had scraped into position around the
feast, a moment of uncomfortable silence hung over the cozy
room. Annie and Drew looked at each other. Who would lead in
prayer? They never prayed before meals at home.

"It is Christmas," said Mr. Pipes, nodding for emphasis with
each word. "The celebration of the birth of Christ the Lord. Let
us pray."

❖ ❖ ❖

Baked ham and roasted potatoes drowning in melted butter,
creamy sweet potatoes spiced with cinnamon, stuffing, and savory gravy soon found its way onto plates and into stomachs as
they feasted together. When they could eat no more and dishes
were cleared away, Annie made a pot of tea and served plates of
shortbread and chocolate for anyone who had room.

"Pass the chocolate, please," said Drew, for the third time.
"Hey, Dad, there's a lake nearby."

"There is?"

"Yeah," said Drew eagerly. "And how about if we men go ice
fishing tomorrow morning—early?"

This was discussed for several minutes with Mr. Pipes explaining how it was done. The caretaker had offered Drew hooks,
line, and a hole cutter, as well as advice on the best spot to fish on
Lake Carter. It was settled.

"You know, I'm really sorry," said Annie and Drew's mother, "that we couldn't bring along any of the gifts."

"Would have taken a cargo plane," mumbled the children's stepfather.

"That's okay," said Annie. "I just wish I had my gifts to give Mr. Pipes and all of you."

"Ah, yes, everyone loves gifts," said Mr. Pipes, leaning forward and looking intently at Annie and Drew's parents. "Have you ever wondered, Mr. Willis, why we offer gifts to one another at Christmas?"

Annie and Drew's stepfather blinked several times and set his teacup on the table. "Frankly, I've never given it much thought," he said. Then laughing, he added, "I always assumed it was a conspiracy started by children and encouraged by toy stores."

"There is that," agreed Mr. Pipes, laughing along with him. "But, of course you know Christmas is the celebration of the historic birth of Jesus Christ, Whom Holy Scripture describes as the 'indescribable gift.'"

Annie bit her lip and looked at Drew.

"So you are suggesting," said Mr. Willis, looking sideways at his wife, "that gifts given at Christmas are some sort of symbol of this Jesus?"

"Oh, that can't be the reason," said Mrs. Willis with a toss of her head.

"It doesn't seem very logical that God would give human beings a gift," agreed Mr. Willis. "Besides, I thought most religions were about humans giving gifts to God. You know, to pay for imagined sins, and all that."

"Precisely, my dear sir," said Mr. Pipes. "You could not be more correct about the uniqueness of Christianity. Like no other religion, the Bible declares men righteous—"

"Men and *womyn*," interrupted Mrs. Willis, frowning at the old man. "Or, *persons*; could we be more inclusive, here?"

"Oh, to be sure, madam," said Mr. Pipes, "The Scripture declares anyone who believes, righteous on the basis of Christ's perfect righteousness. For Christ's sake, He washes repentant sinners' sins away and gives them—one and all—the gift of eternal life. Every other religion declares that you are capable of goodness and that God accepts you based on gifts of good works given to Him. Whereas, the Christian Gospel tells us the truth about ourselves: no one is capable of true goodness."

"Hold on a minute," said Mr. Willis. "Are you suggesting that I, who profess no religion, cannot be good without believing in your Christianity?

"So, you admit that there is a difference between goodness and badness?" said Mr. Pipes, his eyebrows rising with his enthusiasm.

"Of course I do," said Mr. Willis. "Who doesn't?"

"Ah, but on what basis do you decide what is good and what is bad?" replied Mr. Pipes.

Mr. Willis opened his mouth to speak, but for a moment no sound came out.

"Well, I feel that whatever is good for me—is good," said Mrs. Willis. "But I'd never impose my ideas of goodness on someone else—and you shouldn't either."

"Hey, that doesn't make—" began Drew.

Annie drove her elbow hard into his rib cage and gave him a look that said, "Not another word; we've tried our way; let Mr. Pipes speak."

Mr. Willis looked at his wife and frowned. He met Mr. Pipes's eager gaze for a moment and looked away, blinking uncomfortably as the inconsistency of her words—and his own beliefs—began to sink in.

"I-I think we just sort of know what's good," he stammered with a shrug.

"Scripture calls that 'the law of God written on the heart,'" replied Mr. Pipes, reaching for his Bible. "But we, none of us, likes submitting to God's law. In fact, Scripture teaches, what every sinner who honestly examines his heart knows, that we are enemies of God and His law. We are sinners, through and through, desperately in need of Christ, the gift of God and the only Savior of sinners."

⊠ ⊠ ⊠

For the next hour, while Annie and Drew listened, Mr. Pipes answered questions and reasoned with the children's parents from his Bible. Drew, who had seen Mr. Pipes urge the truth on unbelievers before, twisted a clenched fist into his palm in excitement as he looked at Mr. Pipes's animated eyes and flushed cheeks. He loves this, Drew thought, watching the old man lick his finger eagerly and turn the familiar pages of his Bible, readying another reply.

Annie eventually stopped biting her lip as she watched the hint of change come over her parents. They're actually listening, she realized; and she sent silent petitions up to her heavenly Father: "Salvation is from You, O Lord," she prayed. "Give them humble hearts and open their blind eyes."

Mr. Pipes paused and studied the children's parents. They looked sufficiently disturbed with what must be the beginnings of a realization of the sore inadequacies of their self-made ideas. He had no intention, however, of entirely humbling them at this point. No, that would never do. After final urgings and a whispered prayer, he turned to the children.

"Annie," he said, smiling, "Your parents look as if another pot of tea might be in order. I shall help you. And Drew, I believe the fire in the Garden Room could use a fresh armload of wood and a bit of a poke. Mr. and Mrs. Willis, do make yourselves comfortable in the Garden Room. We shall have a fresh pot of tea in a jiffy."

⊠ ⊠ ⊠

A few minutes later, before a spitting and snapping fire in the cozy sitting room, Mr. Pipes and the Willis family sat in rocking chairs, sipping tea and talking about Christmas.

"Well, I still wish I had the gifts I made for you, Mr. Pipes, and for everyone," said Annie, at last.

"Perhaps you do," said Mr. Pipes.

"What?" said Annie.

"Why don't you read us the poem you've been working on whilst snowbound," said Mr. Pipes. "No gift would make me happier, and I'm sure your parents would love to hear it."

Annie looked wide-eyed at Mr. Pipes. What would her parents think? They might even listen.

His chair creaking merrily as he rocked, Mr. Pipes steepled his fingers and nodded encouragingly at her.

She opened her sketchbook, tilted it toward a candle to see better, and cleared her throat. After one last look around the room, and after gently pushing Monochrome's curious nose out of the way, she read:

> Great God, compassionate and kind,
> The God who hears my plea,
> You are my Help whose name I fear;
> My Strength forever be.
>
> In you, O Lord, I put my trust;
> Salvation is from you.
> From dawn to dusk I call your name;
> Your mercy's ever new.
>
> All my desire I give to you;
> Pure joy from you does flow.
> For those who call with humble heart,
> Your grace and love will know.
>
> In all your works how great you are!
> I praise you Lord my God.
> Teach me with undivided heart
> To walk where you have trod.[†]

"You wrote that, Annie?" said her father.

[†] This hymn was actually written by ninth-grade student Anne Stopoulos.

"Did you learn how in school?" asked her mother. "No, that couldn't be it. Did Mr. Pipes teach you how to do it?"

Color rose in Annie's cheeks. "It's still a little stiff. But Mr. Pipes is teaching me—he along with all his old friends."

Joy to the World! The Lord Is Come

Shout for joy to the LORD, all the earth. Ps. 98:4

1. Joy to the world! The Lord is come: let earth receive her King; let every heart prepare him room, and heav'n and nature sing, and heav'n and nature sing, and heav'n, and heav'n and nature sing.

2. Joy to the earth! The Savior reigns: let men their songs employ; while fields and floods, rocks, hills, and plains repeat the sounding joy, re - peat the sound-ing joy, re - peat, re - peat the sound-ing joy.

3. No more let sins and sor - rows grow, nor thorns in - fest the ground; he comes to make his bless - ings flow far as the curse is found, far as the curse is found, far as, far as the curse is found.

4. He rules the world with truth and grace, and makes the na - tions prove the glo - ries of his righ - teous - ness and won - ders of his love, and won - ders of his love, and won - ders, won - ders of his love.

Based on Psalm 98
Isaac Watts, 1719

ANTIOCH C.M.rep.
George Frederick Handel, 1742
Arr. by Lowell Mason, 1836